Rashmi

Flairs and Glairs
Publication House

"Rashmi"

ISBN No: " 978-93-91302-23-8"
1st Edition
Language – English and Hindi

Flairs and Glairs
Publication House
Regd. Under MSME Act.

Disclaimer

This is a work of fiction and solely represent the thoughts of the corresponding authors of the articles. Our editors have tried their best to edit the content of all the authors and check the plagiarism.

All the write-ups in this book are unique and are only published in this book.

In case any plagiarism or error is found, only the author is responsible alone, and not the publisher or the Compilers.

Cover Designing and Book Formatting

Shubham Shah and Ishani Agarwal

Acknowledgment

Dear God, thank you for your blessings,
Also thanks to my family they did everything for me. The compilation of this anthology would have not been possible with the support of Co-authors. A very big thanks to all the Co-authors and the entire team who have been working with us and gave their precious time to us. Special thanks to Shubham Shah and Ishani Agarwal
for guiding me and supporting me although. A good editor makes an ordinary book attractive, thank you Grishma Ninave for doing that. And also thanks to Garima Batra and Shivangi
Jaiswal for helping me get co-authors for this
anthology. And lastly, I Thank "Flairs and Glairs" whole team for helping me.
Thank you all of you for being there.

Co Author

Shubham Shah (Founder Flairs and Glairs)
Ishani Agarwal (Co-Founder Flairs and Glairs)
Riya Rashmi Dash (Compiler)

1. Kalamkaar
2. Shweta
3. Vaibhav Gupta
4. Anand Jain
5. Monisha.T
6. Riya Mishra
7. Padma Srivastava
8. Remya R Pillai
9. Christy Gnana Deepa. J
10. Nirali Rana
11. Prasad Dev
12. Suchismita Ghoshal
13. Sakshi Gupta
14. Rashmi Baweja
15. Urvi Gajjar
16. Krishna Motwani
17. Jayashree Sahoo
18. Diksha Motwani
19. Mausam Agrawal
20. Priya Das
21. Srishty Singh
22. Hema Kirthiga J
23. Ananya Mohanty
24. Anmol Chugh Dildard

25. Swagatika Senapati
26. Nafil Farzana Fathima
27. Lopamudra Sarangi
28. Shivani Kumari
29. Mahi Adlakha
30. Abhishek Mishra
31. Preetam Kumar Khatua
32. Rohit Gupta
33. Archishman Satpathy
34. Surekha Wankhede
35. Ganesh Sadashiv Patil
36. Meetu Thaploo
37. Riddhi Gupta
38. Vedika Shukla
39. Pankaj Grover
40. Kirti Goel
41. Anshuk Dwivedi'ranghin
42. Nilanjana Sarkar
43. Arun Pratap Singh
44. Meetu Chopra
45. Sonali Meher
46. Dikshita Singh
47. V.Dhanashree
48. Rushmi Raj.Amarthaluri
49. Sabene Rizvi
50. Somya Tyagi
51. Mani Prasad Kar
52. Pratham Mittal
53. Chirag L Sagar

Shubham Shah

(Founder- Flairs and Glairs)

Shubham Shah, an entrepreneur at “Flairs & Glairs” a brand with dynamics in events organizing and cultural educational pan INDIA, is a 26yrs old guy who recently has entered the digital platform of imprinting emotions. He has initiated with his own open mic platform to help budding poets and aspiring writers under his brand named as “Teekhe Zasbaaat”

He is a commerce graduate from the Bhagalpur City of Bihar.
He states Writing has impersonated him since childhood and he has now been writing for over a decade!
Cooking, on the other hand, is his passion! He also mentions, trying out new things just tickles him!
When asked sir, Why SPICY EMOTIONS?
He smiled and added, "agar jasbaat teekhe na ho toh wo jasbaat kahan" Spices are all that blends! So do his words!
As a chef, he presents to you his dish! Hot and freshly served! Taste it! Feel it! Enjoy it! You can also find his writing in the Book "Teekhe Zasbaaat" and 50+ Co-authored anthologies. With his passion to explore opportunities across Platforms, he is working with keen devotion and We wish him all the very best for his future ventures.
He is Featured in the International Magazine DeMode for his upcoming solo novel.
He is Approved by Ne8x for its Lit Fest, and is a Golden Star Awards 2020 Winner.
He is a India Book of Records Holder for his Anthology Satrang, and has the Grandmaster title by Asia Book of Records, for the same.
He has also been featured in Prabhat Khabar, Dainik Jagran, and a lot of other Newspapers in Bihar for his achievements.
He has been a proud co-author to
India Book Of Records (Title- Black)
World Book Of Records (Title -15 Wonders of Poetries)
India Book Of Records (Title - Aaina)
Vajra World Records Holder (Title - Gustakhi Maaf Hai)
High Range of Records Holder (Title - Gustakhi Maaf Hai)
Indian Book of Records
(Title - Road from Worst to Best)

Share your reviews on his

INSTAGRAM
@spicy_emotions
@shubham4shah
Or via email on
shubham2shah@gmail.com

To stay tuned to his work and opportunities follow his business Handles

INSTAGRAM FACEBOOK YOUTUBE

@flairsandglairs
@teekhezasbaaat

WEBSITE:
https://flairsandglairs.in/
https://flairsandglairs.com/

Ishani Agarwal

(Co-Founder- Flairs and Glairs)

Ishani Agarwal hails from the City of Joy, Kolkata.
She is the co-founder of her Community "Teekhe Zasbaaat" and Flairs and Glairs Publication.
Been a Compiler for 45+ Anthologies, she is in the process for more. Co-authored in 150+ Anthologies. She is a India Book of Records Holder, a Vajra World Records Holder, a High Range of Records Holder, an OMG Book of Records Holder, a Bravo Record holder, a Forever Star Book of World Records and an Indian Book of Records Holder.
Approved by Ne8x for its Lit Fest 2020, and Literary Icon 2020. Also a Golden Star Awards Winner 2020.
She has also been awarded with India Star Republic Award 2021, a part of She Awards by Awards Arc and Winner of Nari Samman 2021 by Literoma.

She is also selected as Best Achiever of the Year by AwardsArc and Most Challenging Compiler Award by Spectrum Awards.
She got her first solo Published,a solo Compilation consisting of first 750 contents of hers, titled "Hand That Burnt While Healing".

She has been featured by the National Magazine "Taree Zameen Par" with the title 'unstoppable'.
Also featured in the International Magazine DeMode for her upcoming solo novel, she is proud to write on social issues, and is happy with the love she is receiving.
Connect with her on Instagram: @Ishani_agarwal_quotes / @compilations_so_far

Compiler
RIYA RASHMI DASH

She is Riya rashmi dash presently pursuing her BBA from KIIT University, Bhubaneswar. She is Selenophile, loves to enjoy every small moment of her life, and is a wanderlust. She is a writer and started her passion 2 years back and also aspires to be future HR Manager. She has worked in more than 100 anthologies as co-author and compiler of 6 books till now and more ongoing. She is also the Author of her solo book"Waiting to Exhale"She is also been part of national magazines, featured in author interview, part of world record books. She is the Founder of The Opus Coliseum and is happy as her life is turning out now and hopes this continues as such.

Insta- _riyaa_rashmi

Kalamkaar

This is Kalamkaar. He is from Uttrakhand bought up in Meerut(Up). His hobbies are reading and writing. His interest is in writing. He love writing. He is part of 295 +Anthologies as Co-Author. He won 290 + Certificate in Writing, He Start writing 29 February 2020. He is part of 2 anthology as Co Author going for record and He is omg record holder as Co - Author of Book Called Laposia. He is part of 4 international Anthologies as Co - Author. He is simple and people observer. He believes in Karma.

INSTAGRAM:- Kalamkaar51

मान भी जाओ

क्यों मुझसे नाराज़ हो, किस बात का बुरा लगा जो चुप चाप हो!
वैसे तो तुम बाते बहुत करते हो मुझसे, अपने दिल का हर हाल बताते हो!
कभी दिखाते हो अपनी चित्रकला कभी बहुत सुरीला गाते हो!
मुँह फुलाए क्यों बैठे हो, क्या बात क्यों नहीं मुझसे कहते हो!
कोनसी बातसे तुम आहात हो,लादू वो सब चीज़े जो तुम्हारी लेने की चाहत हो!
लाडो हो मेरी दिल का मेरा टुकड़ा हो!
किस बात से नाराज़ हो बता दो चाहें सुना दो अपने दुखड़े को!
आज तुम्हारी हर बात सुनूंगा, पूछो जो मुझसे अपने दिलकी हर अनकही तुमसे बात कहूंगा!
चुप मत रहो कुछ तो कहो जो मेरी गलती हैं वो तो मुझसे साझा करो!
तुम्हारा चुप रहना मुझे खलता हैं, चाहें हर किसी को चले मगर जब तुम बात नहीं करती जो मुझे नहीं चलता हैं!
तुम्हारा मुझे परेशान करना बात बात पर हसना बहुत अच्छा लगता हैं!
चुप्पी अपनी तोड़दो नाराज़गी अपनी छोड़दो बात करो हमसे और मुस्कुराकर हमको दिखा दो!
जो पसंद की चीज़े हैं वो मैं लेऊँगा तुम्हारी एक हसीं के लिए सब कुछ कर जायूँगा!

खुशी

मिलता हु जब तुमसे आती चेहरे पे हसीं हैं !
करता हु तुम्हारे लिए कुछ भी मिलती मुझे उससे खुशी हैं !
तुम्हारे साथ वक़्त बिताना अच्छा मुझे लगता हैं !
झूठे हैं सब तुम्हारा एहसास सच्चा लगता हैं !
तुम्हारा मुझे मूड के देखना मेरा दिल खुश होता हैं !
जाती हो दूर तब दिल मेरा बहुत रोता हैं !
तुम्हारी तन्हाई से दिल में दर्द होता हैं !
तुम तब मेरी छोटी-छोटी चीज़े याद रखती हो मिलती मुझे उससे खुशी हैं !
हसती हो तुम जब मेरे चेहरे पे खिलतीं हसीं हैं !
जाहा हो तुम मेरे लिए सुकून वही हैं !

Shweta

She is Shweta student of life. She loves to travel and wants to live in the hills. She loves to write what she experience. She is a finance student who loves physics more. She is a photographer too. The Pantomath.

INSTAGRAM:- fighting_cages

Change is not an Anchor
We all have a fear of change,
Because it is not within the known range
We feel safe in the old comfortable cage.
Everyone wants to be a ranker,
Because change is not an Anchor .

Just imagine how much courage Aryabhata had at that time,
When speaking against the society was a crime,
Without Zero the numbers are only nine.
I want to ask how many of us are ever taught,
By our parents and teachers that miracles happen .
We all have a reference point which is already achieved by us or someone else.
We all want to know about others' action,
As a different idea comes in, have you ever noticed your reaction .
Due to this how many people have sacrificed their dreams,
Their soul just screams,
Which remains unheard,
By this cruel herd.

The poems I write are like small rocks in the mighty ocean.

Change is not an Anchor.

Vaibhav Gupta

.This is Vaibhav Gupta belonging to Kanpur, UP. He is a graduate and had worked in hospitality department . He has keen interest in poetries and stories. He has recently authored the e-novel "it happened in delhi" and is working on few more. Besides, He has been actively participating on events those lead him to his passion.

INSTAGRAM:- thevaibhav_gupta

Destined together

Guzra main aaj fir un raaho se teri,
Kho jati thi jaha tum banho me meri..
Tanha sadko pe chalte huye,
Maine tumhe mudh ke dekha hai..
Yaado me teri khoke,
Panchhi ban hawa me udte dekha hai..

Yeh bat nahi hai khayalo ki,
Mulakat hai kuch purane saalo ki,
Jis raah me tum mera hath pakad ke chalti thi,
Julfe teri bhi hawaao me ud machalti thi..

Hamein dekh ke khoya ek duje me,
Log bhi kuch jalte se they..
Kaise ham hai is kadar khoye ek duje me,
Soch har aashiq ke dil machalte they...

Kya hota agar tum mili na hoti mujhe,
Kya hota agar tum ban na mujhse karti..
Rah jati ek Kahaani adhuri,
Ya shayed afsos mohabbat karti..

Maine tumhari ankho me khokar tumko paaya hai,
Knona hi to nhi tha tumhe bas,
Isiliye duniya se tumhe churaya hai..
Is khata ki ab saza do mujhe,
Chupa ke apni baanhon me,
Nazro me chupa lo mujhe…

Anand Jain

ANAND JAIN is a good writer from FAZILKA, PUNJAB
He has completed his GRADUATION in commerce stream. From Panjab University.
He has been writing poetry for 3 years as his passion. With the help of sister (sapna jain) and brother (Rakesh jain).
He wants to be a successful banker in future.
He is a founder of ROBIN HOOD ARMY, FAZILKA (NGO).
INSTAGRAM:- Anand_jain_12

लोग

बीते दिन की याद दिलाने आते हैं,
कुछ लम्हें बस आग लगाने आते हैं।

इंटरनेट का युग है अब तू इश्क़ न कर,
तुझको तो बस ख़त भिजवाने आते हैं।

मैंने इश्क़ में सब कुछ अपना खो डाला,
घर से बस ऐसे ही ताने आते हैं।

कोई नहीं सुनता है मुझसे मेरा ग़म,
अपनी-अपनी सब बतलाने आते हैं।

प्यार-मोहब्बत की बातें सब झूठी हैं,
लोग यहाँ बस दिल बहलाने आते हैं।

तुम और मैं

तेरी बातों में गोते लगाए,
तेरी आँखों को मोती बताए, ये आनंद

तेरा हँसना ग़ज़ल में मिलाए,
तेरे रोने पे तुझको हँसाए, ये आनंद

तेरी बातों में उर्दू मिलाए,
तेरे चेहरे पे हिंदी सजाए, ये आनंद

तेरे दिल को शब्दों से छू जाए,
तेरी पलकों पे नज़्में रख जाए, ये आनंद

तू ना हो, अधूरा हो जाए,
तेरे होने से पूरा हो जाए, ये आनंद

Monisha.T

She is Monisha. A daughter of Thirunavukkarasu and Reena. She is currently lived in Villupuram.

She is 18 years of age. She done her Bachelor degree in Physics.

She participate more than 50 anthology as a co-author.

In her every write-ups contains one beautiful concept.

Her words are coming from her kind heart.

She love herself very much.

INSTAGRAM:- monisha_t_official

No Problem

Life is like an endless search
We must be running without rest…
We are searching without knowing
What to look for…!
We are running even though
We have reached the goal…!
Why should we strive like this..?
We have different goals but
The end is Money…!
We are running like this for just to make
Happy to that organ stomach…!
If no one in this world had a stomach
There would be no problem here..!

Riya Mishra

रिया मिश्रा का जन्म उत्तर प्रदेश के भदोही जिले में 31 जुलाई सन् 2000 को हुआ। इनकी आरंभिक शिक्षा हैदराबाद में हुई। नटखट नामक साप्ताहिक पत्रिका ने इनकी रचनाओं को उड़ान दिया। भारतीय समाज में जो घटित हो रहा है और घटित होने की प्रक्रिया में जो कुछ गुम हो रहा है इनकी कविताओं में उसकी प्रभावी पहचान और अभिव्यक्ति देखने को मिलती है। रिया की बिम्बधर्मिता पर पकड़ तो अच्छी है ही, साथ ही दृश्य बंधों को सजीव करने की इनकी भाषा भी सशक्त है।

ये प्रकृति प्रेमी है और समाज में चल रही कुरीतियों का खुलकर विरोध करती है। रिश्तें,वो अंजान राहें,बिन सोशल मीडिया का जमाना, इज़हार, गणतंत्र का पर्व,ज़िन्दगी का सफर,सुकून की तलाश
इनकी प्रमुख रचनायें है। इसके अतिरिक्त इन्होंने कई राष्ट्रीय तथा राज्य स्तरीय संगोष्ठी में भी भाग ले चुकी है। वर्तमान में ये सेंट मैरीस सेंटेनरी डिग्री कॉलेज की बी.कॉम तृतीय वर्ष की छात्रा है। ये कलेक्टर बनना चाहती है।

INSTAGRAM:- Riya3172000

हम दोनों बैठें थे महफ़िल में।
बातें बनाते हुए।
उन्होंने हमारी तरफ मुस्कुराकर क्या देखा।
हमें उनसे इश्क़ हो गया।

ना जाने मूक की भाषा में ,
आँखों ही आँखों में।
उन्होंने अपने दिल की बात क्या कह दी।
और हमें उनसे इश्क़ हो गया।

कातिलाना सा अंदाज़ उनका था।
चेहरे पर नूर था चाँद सा।।
हमने जैसे ही देखा उनकी आँखों में,
दिल मेरा जोरों से धड़कने लगा।
और हमें उनसे इश्क़ हो गया।

कुछ ही क्षणों में उन्होंने।
दिल के कोरे कागज़ पर।
मोहब्बत की मसरूफियत जो दे दी।
दिल का हमारे करार लूट गया।
और हमें उनसे इश्क़ हो गया।

खुदा करें, मेरी दुआँ कुबूल हो जाएं।
मेरा महबूब,मुझें मिल जाएं।
देखकर उसे मैं उसके सीने से लग जाऊँ।
तमन्ना है दिल की, सनम मैं तुम्हारी हो जाऊँ।।

हाथ थामकर तू मेरा उम्र भर का साथ दे दे।
हसरत है दिल की ,कि मेरे हाथो में तू अपना हाथ दे दे।।
तेरे कंधे पर सिर रखकर यूँही बैठी रहूँ मैं,
और तुझमे ही कही गुम हो जाऊँ।।
काश! सनम मैं तुम्हारी हो जाऊँ।

बैठें रहे हम यूँही घंटो तुम्हारे साथ।
और जुल्फे सवारती रही हर पल तुम्हारे हाथ।
तेरी निगाहों में देखती मैं तेरी दुनियां में खो जाऊँ।
काश! सनम मैं तुम्हारी हो जाऊँ।

खुदा करें, मेरी दुआँ कुबूल हो जाएं।
मेरा महबूब,मुझें मिल जाएं।
देखकर उसे मैं उसके सीने से लग जाऊँ।
तमन्ना है दिल की, सनम मैं तुम्हारी हो जाऊँ।।

हाथ थामकर तू मेरा उम्र भर का साथ दे दे।
हसरत है दिल की ,कि मेरे हाथो में तू अपना हाथ दे दे।।
तेरे कंधे पर सिर रखकर यूँही बैठी रहूँ मैं,
और तुझमे ही कही गुम हो जाऊँ।।
काश! सनम मैं तुम्हारी हो जाऊँ।

बैठें रहे हम यूँही घंटो तुम्हारे साथ।
और जुल्फे सवारती रही हर पल तुम्हारे हाथ।
तेरी निगाहों में देखती मैं तेरी दुनियां में खो जाऊँ।
काश! सनम मैं तुम्हारी हो जाऊँ।

हम दोनों बैठें थे महफ़िल में।
बातें बनाते हुए।
उन्होंने हमारी तरफ मुस्कुराकर क्या देखा।
हमें उनसे इश्क़ हो गया।

ना जाने मूक की भाषा में ,
आँखों ही आँखों में।
उन्होंने अपने दिल की बात क्या कह दी।
और हमें उनसे इश्क़ हो गया।

कातिलाना सा अंदाज़ उनका था।
चेहरे पर नूर था चाँद सा।।
हमने जैसे ही देखा उनकी आँखों में,
दिल मेरा जोरों से धड़कने लगा।
और हमें उनसे इश्क़ हो गया।

कुछ ही क्षणों में उन्होंने।
दिल के कोरे कागज़ पर।
मोहब्बत की मसरूफियत जो दे दी।
दिल का हमारे करार लूट गया।
और हमें उनसे इश्क़ हो गया।

Padma Srivastava

She is Padma Srivastava born and brought up in varanasi. Varanasi is not only a birth place for her. She is very deeply in love with varanasi, it is her first love and she wants to connect with it till her last breath. She is a student of Pg from Archaeology from Banaras Hindu University with it she is also a good writer and singer. She became graduated from Banaras Hindu University, Varanasi. She started her career in writing as a co _author since July 2020 from flairs and glairs publication. Now she has been co _author of several anthologies.

INSTAGRAM:- _s_unknown_feelings

इश्क़ - ए बनारस

हर रूह में बसती है आहट उसकी
घाटों पर कई रातें गुज़ारी है
माथे पर महाकाल का भस्म
और काशी जान से प्यारी है।।
शिव जटा की गंगा जहां उतरती,
दिल में बसती जहां मन्दिर की मिट्टी
हर कण, हर सांस में बनारस और
हर रुह में महादेव अविनाशी,, हम वहां के वासी हैं
कर्मस्थली है बनती लोगों की,,
हमारी है जन्मस्थली भी, यहीं वो पवित्र नगरी काशी है
हर कण है साँसों में समाई हुई,,,
रक्षक जिसके स्वयं महादेव जटाधारी है, ,,
हर दिन मानो स्वर्ग हो उतरा धरती पर,
वो स्वप्न से भरा हर शख्स ईश्वर का आभारी है
हर दिन नज़र उतारो तो भी पड़े कम,
हो अंधेरा तो भी उजाले से भरी हर एक दीवारी है,
लोग करते जहां मरने की इच्छा है
जीवन मिला वही से तो अब कर्म करने की बारी है
गलत ना हो कभी किसी शर्त पर हो हर कुछ
न्यौछावर न्याय पर, अब ये हमारी ज़िम्मेदारी है
महाकाल तो है ही हर धड़कनों में बसते
वो जो धड़कती है ना हर पल दिलों में
हर रग में खून सी गंगा बनकर
वो अपनी काशी जान से प्यारी है।।

Remya R Pillai

Remya is the coauthor of over 10+ anthologies. She is from kerala and is pursuing her bachelor degree in physics at TKM college of Arts and Science,Kollam.She is very ambitious, confident and determinant in achieving her goals. She has a great passion in writing as well as dancing. She is a vigorous reader and she is an ardent fan of Nikhita Singh. She likes to transfer her ideas and her emotions in the form of words. She beleives that a pen and paper is the way to her heart and she hopes to help others in finding solace in her writings. Her writings mainly portray the theme of love, lost love, heartbreak, dreams, inspirational,nature and womenhood.

INSTAGRAM:- remzz456

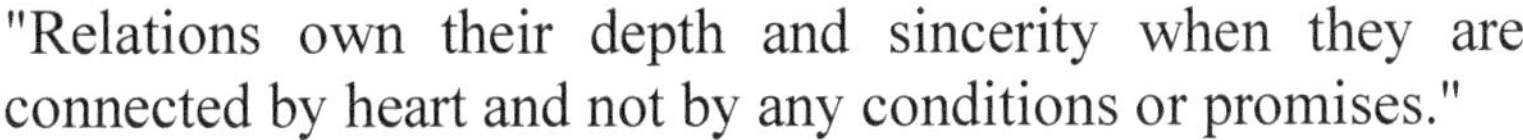

"Relations own their depth and sincerity when they are connected by heart and not by any conditions or promises."

"Every beautiful thing is just an illusion. When the magical spell in it fades, everything begins to disappear. Let it be things, people or some irreplaceable relations."

"In today's world, people should be kept at a distance. Because, the more you remain detached from people, the more happy and safe your heart would be."

"It is the irony of life;
you get attached and then it hurts, and then you get detached and those memories hurt you more."

Christy Gnana Deepa. J

Christy Gnana Deepa , writer pursuing her Undergraduate in English literature in Madurai, Tamilnadu, India. She is a compiler of two anthologies, SECLUDED HEARTS and THE ARDENT HEARTS. Moreover, she is a co-author of more than 25 Anthologies. A writer by passion and a literarian by profession.

INSTAGRAM:- ___budding___writer

1. I'm mad with you still..
because,
you're my crazy Insane!
you're the heart of my life!
without you I'm lifeless…

2.Quality Of Life

Never drop out till you give your best !! Be a fire and never retire.

3.My Beauty is not in my face; it is in my heart....
I'm my own angel!!

4.Open-Mind

If you are open hearted you can win everyone's heart !

Nirali Rana

So Nirali Rana's here... From Vadodara, Gujrat...
She's is 18 years old... Nd science student...
She want to become future Dr...
She just likes to write something new and innovative...
She likes to listen music, sing a song...
She just Love herself the way she want..

INSTAGRAM:- loveyourself1503

Khwaabon Ki Duniya...

चाहने वाले तो बहोत हैं,
पर मेरी चाहत सिर्फ़ वो एक हीं हैं...
समजने वालें तो बहोत हैं,
पर समझाने वाला सिर्फ़ वो एक हीं हैं...
दर्द देने वाले तो बहोत हैं,
पर उस दर्द को अपना पता बताने वाला सिर्फ़ वो एक हीं हैं...
प्यार करने वाले तो बहोत हैं,
पर प्यार निभाने वाला सिर्फ़ वो एक हीं हैं...

Pyaara Dost..

प्यार की तलाश में थी कब से मैं, और
वहां, एक प्यारा सा दोस्त मिल गया...
समझने वाले की कमी थी जीवन मे मेरे, और
वहां, हर ग़लती पर प्यार से समझाने वाला मिल गया...
सोचती थी की आकर कोई हाथ थामे मेरा, और
वहां, एक पागल ने जींदगीभर का साथीदार बना दीया...
रोना तो मानों भूल हीं गई हो जिंदगी में अपनी; क्यूंकि
वहां, हर पल, हर घड़ी, हसाने वाला जो मिल गया हो मुझे...
न हुआ कभी, कोई उतना परेशान मेरे लिए; और
वहां, उसने जता दी एक दिन में हीं चिंता मेरे लिए...
न की दुनियां के सामने कभी तारीफ़ उसने मेरी, क्यूंकि
वहां, #बड़ी_पागल का पुरस्कार जो दे दिया हो मुझे...
न आने देंगे कभी किसी को दोस्ती के बीच में हमारी,
क्यूंकि यारी हैं ही इतनी पक्की हमारी...
समजते हैं लोग पागल प्रेमपंछी हमे; और
वहां, हम दोस्त हीं बेमिशाल हो गए...
प्यार की तलाश में थी कब से मैं, और
वहां, एक प्यारा सा दोस्त मिल गया...

Prasad Dev

His name is Prasad Dev born in Buldana, Maharashtra, India. He had completed his graduation in Bsc. Agriculture from Dr. Panjabrao Deshmukh Krishi Vidyapeeth, Akola, Maharashtra, India. He is a business owner. Currently he is pursuing Diploma in Network Administration from Jetking Swargate Learning Centre in Pune. He like to write to because he love playing with words .He like them arranging them in order to create something meaningful. He love portraying his thoughts and feelings through his words.

INSTAGRAM:- authorprasad
Prasaddevquotes

"Nature" Is What We See.

"Nature" is what we see—
The Hill—the Afternoon—
Squirrel—Eclipse— the Bumble bee—
Nay—Nature is Heaven—
Nature is what we hear—
The Bobolink—the Sea—
Thunder—the Cricket—
Nay—Nature is Harmony—
Nature is what we know—
Yet have no art to say—
So impotent Our Wisdom is
To her Simplicity.

Mother O' Mine

If I were hanged on the highest hill,
Mother o' mine, O mother o' mine
I know whose love would follow me still,
Mother o' mine, O mother o' mine!

If I were drowned in the deepest sea,
Mother o' mine, O mother o' mine
I know whose tears would come down to me,
Mother o' mine, O mother o' mine!

If I were damned of body and soul,
I know whose prayers would make me whole,
Mother o' mine, 0 mother o' mine.

Suchismita Ghoshal

Suchismita Ghoshal from Malda, West Bengal is an internationally acclaimed poet, professional writer, scribbler, published author, professional book critic, storyteller, columnist, former copy-editor at NotionPress Publishing, content writer, creative writing professional, nature lover and a change agent & former Worldwide Ambassadors' Coordinator for Global Youth Leaders Network. She is now a registered member of Global Youth Network. She cherishes her partnership with various publication houses of India & abroad. She enjoys working as a manager at Pen Brew Publishers. Suchismita also aims to heal people with the majesty of her words. She is an environmental activist too who brought reality to her dream as her debut book named "Fields of Sonnet ". Her recent releases are " Poetries in Quarantine" and "Emotions & Tantrums".
INSTAGRAM:- storytellersuchismita

I Am Different Now

I am different now,
I stitch love on my skin
That once was torn apart with the words of hate.
Bright red lipstick stains my lips,
Silently calling the name of your memories.
Here I stand, dreaming you as an empty city
Where I can unveil the secret streets of your mind,
And end up collecting stories from the tender kisses of your lips.
I am different now,
I smell the fumes of alluring tomorrows,
Blending the colours of different moods
Where I portray you in my canvas,
And you portray me in yours.
My heart climbs your sky so high,
And pulls you to reach my walls.
We make a bridge of lights and love,
Where different me see the stars
Of eternity shimmering in your soul.

Sakshi Gupta

Myself Sakshi Gupta, i have done my graduation in BBA , and persuing the mba in marketing , i like to become an ceo and i am having the good marketing skills and have the experience of 1 year in that field . My hobby and Passion is also want to become an writer i like to write about my real feelings based on my mood swings and love to know about people opinion . I have the started my insta page to share my views with others to build my future in this field also.
INSTAGRAM:- Shayaris_by_Sakshi_

Vo Din Bhi Kya Din The

Yu to har kisse ki alag kahaani alag baat hoti hai,
Khaas hote hai magar wo kisse jinme dosto ki yaad hoti hai
Aaye the hum vo bhi yaha , thode darte, thode muskurate, school ke baad ki ek nayi dunia aazmane
Tabhi shoor aya commerce ke bcho ao management courses karlo beta , bahut scope hai
Marketing, selling, manager aur customer ke beech ek yahi to top hai.
Hum bhi bhaag pde fir usi shoor me,
Par kuch hi samay me vo sb bitay hua 3 saal ban gaye,
ab kuch hi palko m ye kshan ek biti hui yaado m badal gay
Wo kshan jo meri zindagi ke anmol pal ban gaye,
Wo kshan jo mere gujre huye ek kal ban gaye,
Kaash un bitay hua lamhoo ko mai ek baar phir se ji pati ,
Kaash aj mai ek baar fir un yaado ki duniya mai dubara laut pati...
Kaash ye beet rha haseen palo ko rok pati, {doraemon ki time machine hmko mil jati} aur un lamho m laut jati,
par ab ye pal tho meri nam aankho ka ek jal ban gaye.
Haan,Wo kshan jo meri zindagi ke anmol pal ban gaye,
Aankho me sapne aur dil me armaan liye,
ek safar me chal pade bina kisi ka hum naam liye,
Raaste me kuch naye chehro se mulakaat ho gayi,
Jese bichade logo se rishtedari hogyi
Haan, ab yahi rishte ek pariwar ban gaye
Wo pal jo mujhe chahne wale mere dost de gaye,
Wo yaadein jo na bhula pane waale kuch log de gaye.

Is anmol safar ki shuruaat hamne saath ki thi,
Marte dum tak sath rhna ki kasan hmna khai thi,
Yaaro mai apna dil ki dhadkan btai thi,
Jaan se pyare yaaro ke saath kitni saari baat ki thi,
Yaaro Zindagi ke sabhi palo ko bhi hamne saath jiya tha,

Kuch palo me khushi aur gam dono ka milan sath kiya tha...
kbhi asuoon ki bhochaar ki thi ,tho kbhi apni haasii ki bochaar kr sbko haasya tha,
Wo kshan jo ab laut ke nahi aa sakte,
Wo pal jaha hum chaah ke bhi ab nahi ja sakte.
kuch hi palko m ye pal yaado m badal gay,
Kuch hi palko mai ye kshan ab ek bita hua kal ban gay
Kuch hi palo mei yaaro ke chehre ek eid ka chaand the,
Vo bhi kya pal tha jab Apne yaaro ke dil ki baat hum bina kahe jaan lete the,
Kaun pasand hai, kisko kya pasand hai or kya nahi smjh jaya karte the
Chhote bade sab jhagdo ke baad sabko mana lete the,
Yaaro k chahra sa hi uska sara gum jaan leta the,
Par ab ye chehra ek bita hua kal ban gaye ,
Canteen aur cafe ki partiya to roz kiya karte the
Paisa kon dega eska liya ek dusre sa jhadga krte the,
Akhir ye yaar the enka sath hum sab khel khelta the ,
Akhir yaaro ke sath roj ek alag hi mehfil hum sajaya krte the,
College aane ka man nahi phir bhi college aaya karte the,
College hota hai pdna ko par pdna ke naam par yha haseenao ke sath ashiqui krte the,
Professor ke lecture ke samay maano alg hi masti chlti the,
Kuch ki kitabo par apni haseena ka kisa hota tha tho kuch apna andar ka kalakaar jagate hua najar ate the,
Professor ko attentive look dena ka alag hi khubi the ,
chlti tho andr bench par apni unki ashiquiya the,
Tabhi tho Kuch logo ko gf/bf aur bakiyo ko teacher bulaya karte the,
exam dene ki to jaise aadat si ho gayi the,
Bina pdhe haar baar exam dena ki adat si hogai the,
Last ke ek ghante m sb pdh liya krte the,
Yaaro ko pkda krte the,
Ek dusra ka hosla baan exam mai aag lgakr aya krte the,
Exam ke baad bs yhi dua Hoti the,

Es baar nikal jaye bs agli baar acha sa pdega
Phir result dekh ke kuch rote to kuch muskuraya karte the,
Ajeeb the ye kshan jisme kuch paye bhi aur kuch khoye bhi,
In kshan ko ek yaad bana bhi ke apne saath le jaungi
Wo kshan jo meri zindagi ke anmol pal ban gaye,
Wo kshan jo ab mera ek bita hua kal ban gaye.

Rashmi Baweja

रश्मी इस कहानी की लेखिका बिल्कुल अपने नाम के अनुरूप ही सबके जीवन को प्रकाशित करती है। रश्मी हरियाणा के सोनीपत जिले की निवासी है। उन्होंने MCA किया है। उन्होंने अपना लेखन कार्य 2016 में प्रारंभ किया। वे बहुत ही स्पष्ट वादी है।वे फेसबुक पर HEART TOUCHING पेज पर भी लिखती हैंlhttps://www.facebook.com/rashmibaweja1993/अलग अलग विषयों पर वे बहुत अच्छा लिखती हैं। उनकी रचनाएँ पढ़कर दिल को सुकून मिलता है। दूसरों के मनोभावों को वे बखूबी समझती हैं। अपने अनुभवों व दूसरों को समझने के अपने हुनर के आधार पर ही वे अपनी रचना लेकर आई हैं। उन्हें इसके लिए बहुत बधाई। आशा है कि उनकी ये रचना सभी को बहुत पसंद आएगी और वे भविष्य में भी ऐसे ही लिखती रहेगी।

INSTAGRAM:- rashmi_baweja13

बहन की खुशी के लिए हर चीज़ भूल जाता है।
उसे तकलीफ हो तो पूरी दुनिया से लड़ जाता है।

हर वक़्त कितना भी लड़े अपनी बहन से।
भाई ही है जो उसकी ख्वाहिशो को पूरा करता है।

कितना भी कहे उसे तेरे जाने के बाद याद नही करूँगा।
पर उसके एक पल ना दिखने से वो बैचैन हो जाता है।

उसकी हर चीज़ को छीन छीनकर उसे खायेगा।
पर जब वो रोने लगे तो उसे सब कुछ दिलाएगा।

कितना भी परेशान करे खुद उसे दिन भर
पर उसे परेशान देखकर वो खुद परेशान हो जाएगा।

ना जाने इस रिश्ते में इतना प्यार कँहा से आता है।
इतनी लड़ाइयों के बाद भी वो उसे दुखी नही देख पाता है।

एक को तकलीफ हो तो दूसरा सब कुछ भूल जाता है।
यही तो वो रिश्ता है जिसमे वो अपनी जान भी कुर्बान कर देता है।

कोई आँसू दे एक कि आंखों में तो दूसरा लड़ने को तैयार हो जाता है।
कितने भी दूर हो एक दुजे से पर दूसरे की तकलीफ वो झट से समझ जाता है।

खुदा का बनाया सबसे पाक रिश्ता कहलाता है।
यही तो है जो एक दूसरे के चेहरे पर मुस्कान लाता है।।

माँ की ममता

नो महीने वो अपनी कोख में पालती है।
अपनी पीड़ा वो किसी को नही बताती है।

बच्चे के हर नखरे वो खुशी खुशी उठाती है।
बच्चे की खातिर वो हर खुशी भूल जाती है।

उसके लिए वो रात रात भर जागती है।
वो परेशान ना हो दिन रात दुआओं में मांगती है।

बच्चे को दर्द में वो देख नही पाती है।
इसलिए हर दर्द वो खुद पर ले जाती है।

पूरा जीवन वो बच्चों के देख रेख पर गंवाती है।
और बड़े होकर वो औलाद उसे एहसान दिखाती है।

जिन बच्चों को वो दस दस बार समझाती है।
बड़े होकर कुछ पूछने पर वो अनपढ़ कहलाती है।

जिन हाथों से वो उन बच्चों को पालती है।
वही औलाद उसे बुढ़ापे में बोझ बताती है।

दुनिया की इस भीड़ में वही है जो प्यार निभाती है।
कितनी भी तकलीफ दे वो फिर भी औलाद की भलाई माँगती है।।

Urvi Gajjar

Urvi Gajjar is a 21 years old young author, graduated in commerce Born in Maharashtra (Mumbai),. Her innovative ideas, loving heart and the enthusiasm towards literature brimmed her personality with the shining pearls of beautiful sayings.

Talking about her, you will see a real spirit and enthusiasm inbuilt in her with a multi-talented personality may it be from drawing a picture or giving reality to writings from simple prompts with true facts and real-life stories with power and you would love to read it for sure.
INSTAGRAM:- _urvi_gajjar__

Dil Ki Aawaz

Mere dil se
Aaj ek awaaz aai

Mera dil roh raha tha
Qki aaj ek baat samj aai

Jo jitna hasata h
Vo utna rulata h

Jo jitna sath nibhata h
Vo kabhi saath chod jayega

Jo abhi apna h
Vo ek din paraya ho jayega

Jo abhi pass h
Vo ek baar dur zarur jayega

Chahe kissise kitna bhi
Pyaar karlo ek din saath zarur chod jayega

Hamesha Jo Karo Vo Dil S Karo

Ek baat yaad rakhna
Agar aapko kissi se baat karni h
To dil se karna
Serf uska dil rakhne k liye nahi

Dil Se Dil Tak

Ek rishta tum tood nai sakte
Jab tum khud tute hue ho
Tut kar bhikar jana kya hota h
Vo pata hota h usse
Jisne khudko tod diya kissi or k liye
Vo dusro ko kabhi nai tutne dega
Qki jo tuta hua h
Vo kya kissko todega
Ya usse juda koi rishta

Krishna Motwani

Krishna Motwani is a Student currently.
She use to pen down her feelings.
She is a moody girl.
She started writing in the month of june,2020.
She writes in her free time.
She writes some motivational quotes or poetries too and practices artworks also.
She lives her life like a bird
As bird flies freely and enjoys life like that she also lives her life freely and enjoy fullest.
INSTAGRAM:- unique__blog_

Love Own-Self!

I love that i am capable to fight with dark phases,
I love myself as i lie but only for my family to have a smile on their faces.

Yes! In some situations I cry,
But again i stand and try.

I don't tell all of my secrets or any incident to all,
I didn't pass sometimes, yes! I fall.

I know how to overcome through sadness,
Life always teaches me to have patience.

I have many problems through which i feel to cry but i don't cry in front of anyone,
I want someone who can understand my emotions but there's no one.

Whatever! I cry, I fail, I lie but i woke again,
Only and only my heart i.e. Me can understand my pain.

I don't care what people thinks of me,
I love as i am, I love me!

Move Ahead!

Dark phases comes to start a new journey with smile on face,
We have solution but we can't find at the moment to fight
with problems.

We have to stay strong,
We shouldn't care if we are not wrong.

We don't have to go back,
Just have to fight and awake.

We all know, through these dark phases we get stressed,
Yes! I know our life is fully messed.

Yes! I know its hard to fight,
But at the end we just feel to hug life tight.

Hardships are part of our journey always,
They will be there to make to strong and find your best ways.

Jayashree Sahoo

Jayashree Sahoo is habitant of ODISHA .
Her writings started on yourquote,notojo and mirakee like writing platforms. You can search her on yourquote by name of Jaya Jayashree . Nowadays She is member of many writing communities and earned a alots of certificates through her writings .
She is Co.author of 140+ anthologies .Also She is Compiler of many anthologies in Hindi ,English and Odia languages . Currently She is working as project head and board member of a reputed publication .
According to her,if you dont express your inner feelings towards someone,then just write those on a paper and making yourself happy for without reason .
Also she has interested in singing ,travelling,photography also. Among of these extra activities She studying Nursing on govt medical and she has an aim for be a RN nurse and good writer .

INSTAGRAM:- mixing_of_emotions

My God Ons

Itna khus nasseb mein kese hosakti hun...
Tum mere pass nehi ho..
Chahte hue v me tumko dekh nehi pati hu
Pr,tum mereko dekh kr muskurate ho..
Har batein na bataein sunlete ho..
Kucch chahun to manse diladete ho..
Kya bolun tumhe bas, ye sochti hun
Itna khus nasseb mein kese hosakti hun..
Bina umidaein sabkucch krlete ho..
Ghar walon se jada tum mereko smzte ho..
Jahn maa janam dekr v kucch galatiyan krleti hein,pr tumse ajtk galatiyan to dur,mere koi bhul v hone nehi dete ho..
Mere hi andar mein rehete ho..
Aur khudko biswa ki raja kehete ho..
Tum itna mahan ho...mere jaan "ONS"
Ye meri sarrer ki atma v pucchti he
,Itna khus nasseb mein kese hosakti hun..
Itna khus nasseb mein kese hosakti hun..
Love u ons
Jay shiv ji

Diksha Motwani

Diksha is a passionate girl from Mumbai, Maharashtra. She loves to pen her feelings. She is introvert but her pen makes her extrovert. She is a writer, singer, artist and a poet!
INSTAGRAM:- radha_1229

Still Am Waiting!

You promised that you will be back very soon,
But you didn't,
I attempted to forget you as you were may be a boon,
But I didn't!

Yes, you are still my morning's first thought,
Yes, I still adore you,
Yes, I still love you.
But may be now, I will not have you.

You were my blooming moon,
You were my shine of darkest days,
unfortunately, you are not mine now,
Yet I still wait for you every single day!

Mausam Agrawal

She is 22 year old girl from Nepal.She has completed her graduation from kolkata and loves writing poems,shayaris and stories.

INSTAGRAM:- mausam.agrawal

Kabhi Socha N Tha

Kabhi socha n tha mulakat unse yun hogi
Karib woh itne hogein ki khamosiyan lab chu legi
Kabhi socha n tha mohbaat unse yun hogi
Ki tasvir unki aanko mai chap jayegi...
Kabhi socha n tha din aisa bhi aayega
Ki bin dekhe unko humko sukoon n aayega
Socha n tha mohbaat iss kadar badh jayegi
Ki bin bole hi sari baatein samaj aayengi.....

Kabhi socha n tha raato ki needein humari bhi udd jayegi. .
Mohbaat main bekudi iss kadar chayegi
Na khud ka hosh rahega na duniya nazar aaayegi
Kabhi socha n tha mohbaat humae bhi ho jayegi....

Kabhi socha n tha koi dil ke itna karib hoga
Jiske bina jeena muskil hoga
Mohbaat bikar jayegi iss kadar hawoo mein
Ki har sama rangin hoga

Priya Das

Priya Das hailing from steel city, Jamshedpur is a teenager with optimistic look to worldly life. She has co authored several anthologies and currently working on a novel. She is a great music lover and admires travel bloggers.
INSTAGRAM:- inexorable_voice

From Bench To Table!

"Pin drop silence"
My ears heard those words
The words I heard years back
And then now again!
But the difference within it
Just blows in my mind
As the vibes passes.

I used to hear it as a student
While seriously digging into the chapter
While my favourite teacher patted on the table
But today I was standing in the same school, same class,
saying same words while patting on the same table
and with the passage of time bench was replaced by the chair
and table.

Srishty Singh

She is Srishty Singh from Dhanbad, Jharkhand. She is 18 and currently doing her btech. Writting is her passion. She writes in numerous formats and in three languages. She has contributed to various anthologies as co author and a part of many writting communities.
INSTAGRAM:- srishty_28_singh

Ishq Ka Chaska

[Format- Ghazal]

Chaska tere ishq ka kuch yu chaa jaaye,
ke us chaand ka bhi guroor sheesh jhukaye.

Talab aisi ke saanson me samaa loon tujhe,
tu hi ibadat me ho tu hi rab ka nazrana laaye.

Khuda se dua bas yahi ki mere hosh me tera nasha,
aur teri rooh me fitoor bas mera mera hi aaye.

Teri saanson ke noor me panah kuch yu paa loon,
ke rooh me basi mohabbat bepannah ho jaaye.

Tera sajda kuch yu karoon....ae mere rehbar,
ankhon me tu hi base " khwab" me tujhe hi paaye

Ishqbaazi

Socho toh barishein bhi raahat ka nazraana laayi hai,
socho toh har ek boond me basi sukoon ki gehrai hai.

Jo khuda ki banayi sabse umda karishma hai jannat
karoon sajda tera hi mannat me bas tu aayi hai .

Ke beghar ho kar bhi kabhi tanhaa na hua,
har maayusi jo bhar gayi teri hi parchayi hai.

Ab hasraton ke daayrein kuch yu behad ho gaye,
ke jo maut se berehem ho wo teri bewafai hai.

Rooh ki nazaakat toh har parindey me tapdeel hai,
mohabbat ki ada ki toh kurbaanii ne dikhayi hai..!!!

HEMA KIRTHIGA J

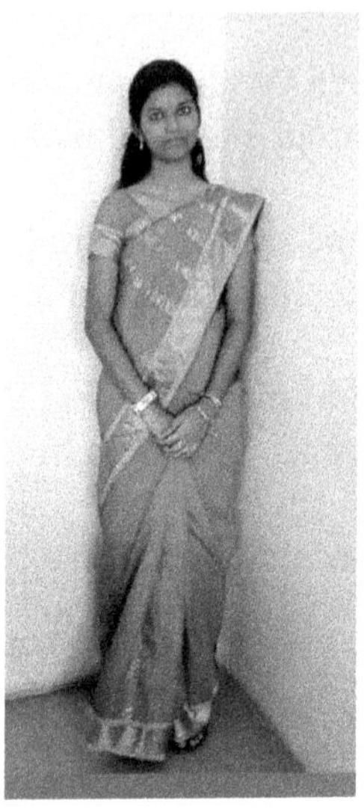

She is Hema Kirthiga J, and her pen name is sparkle. She is professionally a psychologist and passionately a writer. She heals others but writing heals her. She is writer, reader, orator and a believer. She is from Chennai. She lives by the principal of inspire and be inspired. She writes her heart and soul and she deeply believes that the depth of her heart and the nib of her pen are soulfully connected. Writing is an art and she is a proud artist. She loves what she does and loves what she writes.

INSTAGRAM:- the_pen_queen

Inker!

She is a inker,
She inks her live,
She inks her love,
She inks her pain,
She inks her dreams,
She inks her passion,
She inks her tears,
She inks her blood,
She inks her emotions,
She inks her life,
She inks her relationship,
She inks herself,
She inks her success,
She inks her failure,
She inks her trust,
She inks her betrayal,

Ananya Mohanty

Ananya Mohanty hailing from the city of Rairangpur. An author in 75+ anthologies and a compiler also. She is also a record holder in KALAM WORLD RECORD and SPECTRUM INSPIRING INDIAN WOMEN. Writing is like a way to say your feelings out. So I write to express myself . So some of the writing are in real my own stories. My life My story. I love writing for myself. This is also something I wrote from some of my life phase. My much of the writings are on romance, mystery, fantasy, motivation and horror.
INSTAGRAM:- Sweet_devil_lover

My Vampire King

Today I went to the dead forest with my friends for a trip. It's called dead forest coz no one stays alive if they stay there after mid night. Many had gone there out of curiosity but only a few lucky have returned. Many rumors are there that the forest had a door to a magical place which is heavenly as well as deadly at the same time. They said that there are mythical creatures that protect the castle and the Prince from the humans. And me being a student of mythology can't stop myself from coming here. By the way I am Park Amo. I came here with 4 of my friends and we will stay here outside the forest to just monitor the forest at night. After some hours it's already time to start our work as it's 11:30 pm now. And all of my friends are dead tired coz of the fixing of the cameras on the trees to monitor it. Now it's already midnight but we didn't notice anything and soon enough my friends started to fall asleep but I can't so I ended up deciding to take a walk around the forest. After walking some distance I heard a faint melodious sound of flute. And without noticing it I went that way and to my surprise I ended up in front of a cave when I came back to my senses I was already far away from our camp.

As no option left to choose I entered the cave and was mesmerized by my surrounding it was just magical and heavenly and at a few distance I saw a tall figure facing it's back to me and playing that flute. And again my foot started to walk on their own but before I reach near that person, he stopped the flute and so as my foot were, I was just freeze at my spot. When he turned around to face me he was smiling and was so pulchritudinous that I can't take my off of him. But suddenly some images started to flash in my head and I began screaming and completely blackout but before I close my eyes I felt someone holding me and saying " Welcome Home My QUEEN ". And then I was having a dream where I was with that person I saw earlier but we were "VAMPIRES" and then someone attacked us and I came in front of him and got stabbed in my heart with a silver sword and then out of anger he killed and burned all the man there and crying and begging for me to not leave me. And I promised him I will be reborn again to be his queen. And then I shut open my eyes and saw that person beside me. He was crying and I hugged him and said " My Love I am Back ". And after that I asked him to make me his but before that I need to go back and bid goodbye to all. And then after that I am back to MY VAMPIRE KING AS HIS QUEEN.

Anmol Chugh Dildard

अनमोल चुघ दिलदर्द मूल रूप से जालंधर शहर,पंजाब से ताल्लुक रखते हैं। अनमोल जी फिलहाल पंजाब टैक्निकल यूनिवर्सिटी (Punjab Technical University), जालंधर, पंजाब से स्नातक बी. टेक, सिविल इंजिनियरिंग (B.Tech,Civil Engineering) की पढ़ाई कर रहे हैं। प्रस्तुत पुस्तक में अनमोल जी ने मन की भावनाओं को व्यक्त किया है। अनमोल जी पहले बहुत सी पुस्तकों में अपनी रुचि दिखा चुके हैं।

INSTAGRAM:- anmolchugh8383
love_shayri_thoughts

होली

होली एक पवित्र त्योहार है। इसको मार्च के महीने में रंगों द्वारा मनाया जाता है। परंतु आजकल देखा जाए तो इसको लोग रोज़ मनाते हैं: अपनी चतुराई और मतलब से। लेखक ने अपनी इस सोच को कुछ पंक्तियों द्वारा प्रस्तुत किया है।--

होली तो रोज़ खेलते हैं लोग,
गिरगिट की तरह रंग बदलते हैं लोग,
होली तो रोज़ खेलते हैं लोग,
अपने रंगीन चेहरे दिखाते हैं लोग,
होली तो रोज़ खेलते हैं लोग,
अपना मतलब निकालते हैं लोग,
होली तो रोज़ खेलते हैं लोग,
अपनों को ठुकराते हैं लोग,
होली तो रोज़ खेलते हैं लोग,
एक दूसरे को जलाते हैं लोग,
होली तो रोज़ खेलते हैं लोग,
अपनों का फायदा उठाते हैं लोग,
होली तो रोज़ खेलते हैं लोग,
अपनों की पीठ पर ही वार करते हैं लोग,
होली तो रोज़ खेलते हैं लोग,
एक दूसरे को नीचे गिराते हैं लोग..!!

तुम्हारी चुप्पी

तुम्हारी चुप्पी ने सब बयां कर दिया,
मेरे दर्दों को फिर से इतलाह (संदेश) कर दिया,
हम दोनों के रास्ते थे एक जैसे,
ना जाने क्यों;
तुमने अपनी मजबूरी को मेरे नाम कर दिया..!!

तेरी तरफ आते हुए

तेरी तरफ आते हुए,
अपने हालात बताते हुए,
मैंने बहुत ज़ख्म खाए हैं,
तुझे खुदा मानते हुए,
तेरी पूजा करते हुए,
तेरा नाम जपते हुए,
मैंने बहुत ज़ख्म खाए हैं,
तेरी दुआएं करते हुए,
तेरे ख्यालों में मरते हुए,
तेरी यादों में जलते हुए,
तेरी आह में आह भरते हुए,
मैंने बहुत ज़ख्म खाए हैं..!!!

Swagatika Senapati

She is swagatika, currently a student. She loves to write, paint, and dance. She likes to do more creative works and explore herself as well as her talents.
INSTAGRAM:- _art.is.everything_

Memories Of The Year

YEAR 2020...
It's just like a long dream!
Beyond human's imagination!
It has proved that the word impossible,
Don't exist...
Year 2020 is a year of examples...
It declared our results also!
Are you thinking which results?
The results is the examinations,
That we humans we giving
From so many years...

It's a memorable year for all humans...
He will think thrice before his evil deeds…

Nafil Farzana Fathima

Nafil Farzana Fathima is a middle school English teacher by profession and a graduate in Master's in Physics who is also pursuing her Bachelor of Education (2020). Her journey of publishing books started at an age of 12 when her first painting was published in "Thina Thandhi" newspaper. She is a girl who grabs all the opportunities that come her way. She bagged many prizes during her school and college days for various competitions. Being Tamil as her favorite language and subject, she bagged the first prize in Tamil State Level poetry competition under "பாரதியார் கல்வி மேம்பாட்டு மையம்" and "வந்தே மாதரம் மாணவர் தமிழ் மன்றம் தேர்வு". She believed in the power of writing from the bottom of her heart. She strongly believes in a monotheistic religion — "Oneness of God" and is passionate to acquire the knowledge of Islam. She has been working as a co-author in the books "The Miscellany of Odes", "With Love-A 100 Unsent Letter", "The Society of Taboos", "The Hidden Love", "Give Wings to Your Love", "Daily Thoughts", "Self Vibes", "Midnight Melodies", "Tera Shehar", "From the Heart", "Life-A Journey" and also compiled books named, "50 Islamic Poems", "Pour Your Memories" and "You Make My Heart Sing". You can grab those books in all the online platforms. She is also interested in sports and arts, which had made her be a champ in sports until her high school. She always regretted that she could not continue playing sports after her schooling. Apart from this, she had worked as a Vice-president in an Interact-club (2013),had been an Assistant School Pupil Leader (2014) and also a Representative of Rotaract Club (2017). She is preparing herself to publish a solo book in the near future. Way much to grow and glow, her success is only from Allah, who is solely responsible for what she is today. (11:88)

Be A Sunshine!!!!!

Be a bird that flies across the sky,
To achieve what it loves and reach high.
Don't lock your dream in a cage of no where,
Give wings to your love that fly and occupy everywhere.

The trees that shed leaves in autumn,
Are definitely born to a new life in spring.
But don't forget to water the roots,
To keep it alive and shoot.

The busy bee that works hard admires me,
Which fetches nectar from flowers with so much glee.
Dark clouds pour heavy rain,
On the ground without any pain.

Be a sunshine,
That brings rainbow.
Not the sunset,
Which brings darkness.

Be a thunder,
That world wonder!!!
Be a lightning,
That spark without frightening.

Lopamudra Sarangi

Lopamudra Sarangi belongs to Odisha,has completed her 12th boards.She is interested in getting into Civil Services.She is an optimistic girl with smiles and hopes around.She is a debater and also loves to sing,dance and write.She is always ready to explore her capabilities.Her aim is to change the perspective of the society through her writing.

Soul

If I'll be stainless,your worth will upraise among all.
If I'll be substandard,your stature will drop in front of all.
If I'll counsel you,you'll be a considerable man for all.
If I'll dictate you erroneously,you'll be censured by all.
If I'll be disorientated,you'll encounter a gigantic fall.
If I'll be smashed,your bliss will become null.
If I'll be thrilled,you'll earn pleasure even more than all.
But once I split from you,you'll be declared as dead for all.
Just recall,it's me;your soul,
It's my memorandum to you all.

Shivani Kumari

शिवानी कुमारी दिल्ली विश्वविद्यालय बी.ए. द्वितीय वर्ष की छात्रा है। लिखने की वज़ह मालूम नहीं, पर लोगो की लिखावट को पढ़ना और सुनना अच्छा लगता है, और धीरे धीरे , कब लिखना शुरू कर दी मालूम नहीं चला ।और फिर लिखना इनका शौक बन गया, ज़ेहन में चल रही बातो को पन्ने पे उतारने का जरिया बन गया, कुछ अपनी, कुछ अपनों की बातो को बिन कहे किसी से लिख कर सब कह दिया ।

INSTAGRAM:- Meri__syahi

अब मुझसे लिखे जाते नहीं हालात मेरे..
पर मेरी स्याही लिखना चाहती है,
मेरे जज़्बात ,ख़्याल और एहसास।
मैं कैसे इन्हें ना लिखूं..
पाठक ढूंढता है, मेरा अस्तित्व, मेरी सच्चाई और मेरे कुछ अतीत के पहलू मेरी लिखावट में।
मात्राओं की लकीरें अक्सर बयां कर देती है, मेरी पीड़ा को..
वो पीड़ा जो क़ैद हैं, मेरे हृदय के भीतर।

अब मुझसे लिखे जाते नहीं हालात मेरे..
पर लिखूंगी नहीं तो बताऊंगी किसे!
कोरे कागज़ मुझे आकर्षित करते हैं, अपनी ओर
कि छुपाओ ना तुम अपने भावों को,
कर दो प्रकट स्वतंत्र रूप से,
और ख़ुद भी स्वतंत्र हो जाओ, चिंतित परिस्थितियों से।

अब मुझसे लिखे जाते नहीं हालात मेरे..
ख़ुद को लिखना भले छोड़ भी दूं,
पर समाज में मौजूद कुरीतियां अक्सर मुझे उकसाती है, कुछ ऐसा लिखने को,
कि शर्म की कुएं में डुबकी लगाकर, आभास हो उन्हें अपनी करनी पर, सोच पर और अपने भीतर एक शैतान पर।
कौन शैतान, कौन इंसान और कौन भगवान?
अक्सर इसी उलझन में उलझ के रह जाते हैं मेरे स्वयं के विचार।
अब मुझसे लिखे जाते नहीं हालात मेरे।

भूल जाने का तो प्रश्न ही उत्पन्न नहीं होता,
कि कैसे तुम्हें और तुम्हारी स्मृतियों को भुला दूं।
तुम्हारी बातों की गर्माहट
मुझे आभास होती है, आज भी ,हर क्षण।
यें शीत ऋतु मुझे ग्रीष्म के समान लगती है।
तुम्हारी हंसी ऊन के गोले जैसी थी,
जिससे मैंने बुन लिया, एक सुंदर सा "गुलबंद"।
जो सदैव मुझे प्रिय है,
हमेशा मुझे गर्माहट प्रदान करती है।
तुम्हारा रूठना मेरी चाय जैसा था,
जो ठंडी होने पर मुझे भी
मायूस कर जाती थी।
तुम्हारा नटखट सा व्यवहार,
मेरे हृदय को भीतर से ,
एक मासूम सी बच्ची बनाए रखता था,
जो हमेशा अपनी मां का गरम आंचल ढूंढती थी,
छुपने के लिए।
तुम्हारी बातों की गर्माहट, मुझे आज भी आभास होती है।

रक्त से सींच कर
एक "प्राण"बना।
प्राण को महत्व मिला,
पर मिला ना कोई सम्मान
उस रक्त को।
हर माह के 5 दिन
वो बहती रही,शर्मो हया
की चादर ओढ़ कर।
घृणा का पात्र मानकर
दी ना गई उसे कोई इज़्ज़त।
दूर रखा गया उसे
हर अनुष्ठानिक क्रियाओं से।
पर लाल रंग तो चढ़ा है,
हर पवित्र स्थल में।

पवित्रता क्या है?
"लाल रंग"
फिर एक स्त्री के देह से निकला रक्त
क्यों है अपवित्र?
यूं तो स्त्री "देवी" का रूप है,
फिर महावारी अशुद्ध क्यों है?
शुद्ध और अशुद्ध मस्तिष्क का मैल है,
मस्तिष्क और हृदय जैसी सोच रखेगा,
अशुद्ध भी शुद्ध लगेगा।

स्त्री की लिखी हुई कविताओं का इतना महत्त्व नहीं,
क्योंकि वो ना चाहते हुए भी
लिख देती है,, अपनी व्यथा को।
उड़ेल देती है वो ममता अपनी कविताओं में।
वो नहीं कर पाती तुलना
सुंदरता की ,जैसे करता है कोई कवि मोह जाल में फंस कर।
स्त्री के आंसू की तरह ही होती है कविताएं उनकी,
जो दिखते ही नहीं किसी को।
वो कविताएं उन्हीं हाथों से लिखी जाती है जिस हाथ से बनता है,
सजता है, व निखरता है एक घर,, एक स्त्री का।
फिर क्यों नहीं पढ़ता है, कोई स्त्री की कविताओं को।

Mahi Adlakha

Mahi is 15 years old. She belongs to a small town in Rajasthan. She writes as her hobby. She is very happy-go-lucky and very bubbly. She writes out her heart.

INSTAGRAM:- dazzledust_

If You Had A Moon

I'll escape from here very soon,
I'll hear you from the moon,
I wonder if you'll still have complaints,
But you'll forever remain my mains,
I trust not what I hear,
But what the moon said in my ear,
My intention was pure,
I could stay down without any fear,
Only if you had a moon to tell that in your ear.

Are We?

There is a time at all times,
When all of you rhymes,
When the shadow of the sun,
Still brings sunshine,
And the song you murmur perfectly rhymes,
With u, with me,
Or with us,
I hope you stay forever this time,
Dear love, please rhyme,
Or maybe you just take another curve,
Is it just me,
Or are we all in love?

Abhishek Mishra

Abhishek mishra is benevolent person with futuristic vision he is graduated in field of science with a great academic experience having vociferous attitude on podium as well in gatherings, he always enjoys and dedicate himself to writing with great zeal, he belongs to financial capital Mumbai and rooted to Jaunpur of Uttarpradesh. He is strong believer and full of positive attitude,also

He is an active participant in census pragramme of biodiversity survey in goa, Currently he is contemplating for being one of the recognized writer of Republic of India with all possible efforts and grace along with all above he is a passionate cricket lover

He has great smitten for meaningful and veraciuos writeups and always appreciate such works. He thinks that it is books that keep you away from mental health

and best partner for your whole journey.

INSTAGRAM:- Abhishek vision

वक़्त सब ठीक कर देता हैं ।

बिगड़ते रिश्तों को ,
विछड़ते दोस्तों को ,
और बड़े से बड़ा घाव को ,
वक़्त सब ठीक कर देता हैं ।

अनजाने में हुई गलती को ,
मन की कड़वाहट को ,
दिल की दर्द को ,
किसी को भुलाने की कोशिश को ,
वक़्त का मलहम सब ठीक कर देता हैं ।

अपनों से ना मिलने के गम को ,
जूझते हुए ज़िन्दगी को ,
सालों से चले आ रहें विवाद को ,
वक़्त सब ठीक कर देता हैं

बचपन

फूलों के सुगंध जैसा था बचपन ।
परी लोक जैसा था बचपन ।
मम्मी का डाट कर स्कूल भेजना ,
और वापस आते ही हमको राजकुमार जैसा दिखाना ।
ऐसा था बचपन ।
याद तो होगा ही चूरन की पूड़ियाँ , लकड़ी के धोड़े
और मिट्टी के तराजू ,
इनसे ही तो था बचपन ।
सच्चा वाला मुस्कान , और कभी झूठा वाला रोना ,
यू चला बचपन हमारा बचपन ।
सुख दुख क्या होता हैं? ये पता ना होना
बस मस्ती में झूमते रहना वो था बचपन ।।
दोस्ती क्या होती हैं ये पता भी न था ,
फिर भी उनके लिए कुछ भी कर गुजरना ,
ये था बचपन ।।

Preetam Kumar Khatua

PREETAM KUMAR KHATUA, a native of Sambalpur, Odisha. A budding author and an adroit orator. Currently pursuing Bachelor in Dental Surgery in Bangalore. Loves to express heart's beat in words. Probably a romantic man of letters. Feel his poems and get lost in the world of delightfulness. Loves to define the beauty of a girl through words. Believes in works rather than sayings.
INSTAGRAM:- p.p_r_e_e_t_a_m

Friendship

Ankhen khuli to dekha doctoron ki bheed jami hui hai, Family members ke muh se khusi bhi udi hui hai.
Pata chala mujhe cancer hua hai, Do din aur jee loon, yahi dua hai.
Gaur tha mujhe ki do paal aur jee na paunga, Man mai aash thi jate jate hasin geet gaa jaunga.
Uthaya phone, bheja message do logon ko, Likha m jaa raha hoon, ho sake to rok lo.
Dono mai se ek thi meri premika, dusra mera yaar, Zindagi ki nayya wahi lagayega meri paar.
Girlfriend boli “I am busy call you later”, All my hopes and faith got shattered.
Socha tha ayegi milne ek baar mujhse, Par wo to ye bhi na puchi, kahan jaa rha hoon main door sabse.
Dost bola akele kahan jaa rha hai, Bhai ko bhula kar thandi hawa kha raha hai.
Aankh aur dil dono bhar ayi uski baat sunke, Ye zindagi kaise khatam kar doon use bhula ke.
Bolta hai kameena phone ghumake, Ruk jaaaa, milke maze lenge kamar hilake.
Nark bhi jayenge to sath sath nibhayenge, Ye dosti hum kabhi nahi bhula payenge.
Aaj phir dosti baazi maar li pyar se, Kya pyar kabhi mehengi ho sakti hai dosti se?

Beauty Of A Girl

And so adorable your eyes are,
Majestic is your smile, that makes my heart stumble.
I look back at you, even my eyes tremble.
Falling more and more in your love, each time I see you.
Down the heavenly sky, came like a blessing,
O red red rose! So pleasant is you.
When I dream to hold your hand, I say a silent prayer.
That we will be together and together forever.
You gave a reason to smile,
Enriched my life and made it worthwhile.
As I still hold your hand, walking over the golden sand,
I make a promise, we will walk a thousand miles till the end.
I know, it's getting a bit bigger,
I should stop before you pull the trigger.
Its all about the prettified pearl,
This poem portrays the beauty of an adorable girl.

Rohit Gupta

This is Rohit Gupta (Advik),a 19 year old boy born and brought up in Agra,The City of Taj.... He's persuing his bachelor's degree in History from University of Delhi and a budding IAS Officer....His Hobby is writing and starts Writing from schooling.....He believe writing is the best way to express your inner self to the world.... He's a Published Compiler and complied two anthology under the Publication Spectrum of Thoughts.

INSTAGRAM:-

the_hacker_of_heart_ i_write_what_you_feel_09

When your day starts with their Message
nd ends on that....
When you fights for no reason and solved it asap....

When you care for them and worried unless....
When you forget everything like a stranger's mess....

When you are full of anger and burst like an ice....
When you are sad enough and they listen your Unheared cries....

When you said there is no one and your face starts blush....
Then your body denies and your hearts says *Yes you are in Love*….

Archishman Satpathy

Archishman Satpathy, often called "The Enthusiast Writer" is a young dynamic guy from Deogarh, Odisha, is a young lad of 17.
He is the co-author of 300+ Anthologies and Author of the book "LAKEEREIN ZINDAGI KE".
He is the Brand Ambassador of an world record holder antho of NLHF, the Brand Ambassador and the Marketing Head of the Roses and Quills Community, the Coordinator of The Unicorn Tales, the Editor of The Sturdy Writers Community, Chief Operating Head of Gleaming Inscription Community, Chief of Hindi Department of InKadhai Publication, English Jury of Writers Ammulet.
He is the Co-founder of The Peaceful Writers Community and The Writing Gurus Community.
He is currently in 20+ Writing Communities at present.
He won the "Youngest Writer to 200 Anthologies" award by Indian Professional Awards.
INSTAGRAM:- jokerpoet_2882

Writing Became My Love

Writing became my love, when
The adolescent kicked me out
And the teenage started ignoring

Letting the failures to conquer
I was unable to live a life with a life
Leading a fortunate edge of greatness
The slider was rolling in a short knife

Shuttling with the conscience
I started focussing on work
Just because the form now back
Luck is jumping high like a shark

Then the shot cracked and tore
The day and the happiness apart
When I realised the importance
What Writing gave before depart

I Am No More Yours

Today you are not mine anymore
That deepest is that endeavour???

You tried to be controlled right?
Again the same thinking in sight
I must have stopped you from that
That gave you the freedom so apart

We could have resolved the matter
But I have to accept, for mine you don't
For mine , you are no more

We planned for some verses of us
And now left with nothingness
Just the pillars we are followed had broke
The pieces apart are still unable to stroke

I just want that script to be for us
In the golden history of shrine
Yes today the night will be harder
But tomorrow again the sun will shine

Surekha Wankhede

Surekha Wankhede belongs to Orange City, Nagpur, Maharashtra. She is persuing her graduation in B. Pharmacy course from RTMNU University. She writes in every type of genre, which considering where you are reading this, makes perfect sense. She's the best known for English poetry. She writes on every topic, she looks most innocent girl but her mind is filled with lots of creative and interesting stuffs. Passionate about her work, in love with her family and dedicated to spreading joy and light of her uniqueness. She is working as PH and Head Of The Magazine Dept. at The Opus Coliseum Publication. She wrote her magic just like the chemistry.

INSTAGRAM:- nuance_sayings

पापा की लाड़ली बेटी...

पापा की लाड़ली होती है बेटी,
लेकिन वो दिन बड़ा ही दु:ख दायक होता है,
जब उसे विदा करने का दिन आ जाता है।
अपने हाथों से खिलाया है जिसे,
हर कदम पर मुश्किलों से लड़ना सिखाया है जिसे,
दुनिया मे सबसे ज्यादा प्यार करता हूं तुझसे ये एहसास दिलाया है जिसे,
हर बार उसे सबसे अधिक महत्त्व दिया है,
उसकी हर ख्वाहिश पूरी की है,
आज उसे विदा करने का दिन आ गया।

वो पापा आज ये सोच में पड़ गए है की,
मेरी लाडली को क्या उस घर में ढेर सारा प्यार और इज्ज़त मिलेगी जो उसे यहां मिलती हैं।
क्या सब उससे इतना ही प्यार करेंगे की,
वो हमे भी भुल जाएगी।
क्या उसकी हर जरूरत का ध्यान रखा जाएगा।
आज वो सारी यादें वो हर पल को पापा ने अपनी लाड़ली के साथ बिताया है वो याद आ रहा हैं।
और उस याद मे उनकी आंखें नम हो गई है।

Ganesh Sadashiv Patil

This Is Ganesh Sadashiv Patil From Jalgaon,Maharashtra.He Is The Student Of UG In Field Of Pharmacy.He Is Writer And Poet Who Writes 100+ Poetry In Hindi And Marathi Languages.He Has Worked In 10 Anthologies As A Coauthour.He Is Also Been Part Of Pratibha E Magazine.He Is Also Been Part Of Various Poetry And Writing Competitions At National Level.He Loves To Write On Love,Humanity, Motivation And Social Themes. He loves to write down his feelings, his thoughts.He Is The CoAuthor Of 20+ Anthologies.

INSTAGRAM:- gsp9599

प्यार की बाते

बाते करते करते हम दोनो ना जाने कितने पास आ गये है
जुबान पर आ गयी है बात मेरे पर सारी बाते कल करते है
प्यारतो बोहोत है आपसे पर हिम्मत ना कुछ केहने की है
खूबसुरत हो आप इतने की आपको हि देखते हम रेहते है
प्यार हुआ है जबसे हमे आपसे ना जाने ख्वाबो में रेहते है
यादे आती है आपकी हर दिन प्यार का इझहार ना करते है
आज कहुंगा कल कहुंगा बस इसी तरह दिन निकल रहे है
प्यार है आपसे बहोत हमे दिल से बाते हम ना केह पाते है
ना जाने कब वो कल निकलेगा जब हम आपसे बात कहेंगे
राह हम देख रहे है उस दिन कि कब दिलकी ये बाते करेंगे

Meetu Thaploo

Accidental Engineer
Author by heart and Passion .
Writing since She was 13 years old.
She wrote her first poem when She was in 6th grade helped by her mother .
Worked in different sectors of MNC like Telecom ,Aviation,Metro & Education for 10 years and finally ended up to be a full time writer. She Wrote about 72 Anthologies & 1 Solo Book in preparation.
Compiling 14 Books in process on less talked off topics like LGBT , Kashmiri Migration, Sexual Child Assault and Women Orgasm .
She does endorsements for over 11 Fashion brands and Produced a Video Song recently about her Home Land Kashmir "Kashmir Mera Ghar ".

INSTAGRAM:- likh_du

जिस्म से रूह तक जाने मैं वो एक बात नही लगती
आज-कल कि generation कि वो एक रात नही लगती

कम हि समझ आता है हमें ये तुम्हारे जमाने का ये लव आज कल
बातों बातों से जो पी जाते थे हमें अपने पहलू मैं ,तुम लोग वो बात नही समजती |

ये क़िस्सा सच सा शायद तुम्हें लगे भी ना पर महीनों बात नही करके भी जो बातें हो जाती थी तुम वो बात नही समझते

पहली मुलाक़ात मैं लड़का -लड़की का चरित्र देखते थे कितना हंसा सकता है केसे बात करता है
ये आज कल कि तरह पहली मुलाक़ात में साइज़ और position यू लाइक नही पूछते !

हम पहली बार अकेले मैं भी इसने मिले तो May I ,कहके हमें शर्मिंदा नही किया !
जो जिस्मों मैं लगी थी आग उसे हम इबादत सा करते नापाक नही किया ! !

नंगी पीठ पे नाम लिखना और पहचाना, हमारी बेस्ट गेम होती थी |
ये एक रात मैं कितनी बार और केसे का हम हिसाब नही रखते|

निकाह से पहले के 8, और उसके बाद के 7 साल हो गये !
क्यूँकि हम मोहोबतों मैं स्टैमिना नही, विश्वास ढूँढते थे !

रातें तमाम चिरिगो सी जलिए है हमने और उन रातों कि हम बात नही करते !
आज भी सुबह उठ कर हम खुद को देख कर अल्लाह का शूकर करते है !

अपनी रातें बस एक के साथ मुनासिब लगती है हमें ,हम अपने जिस्म, अपनी रात, और बिस्तर कि सिलवटें किसी घेर के साथ share नही करते !!

किसी दूसरे कि video clip और ना कोई Porn
हम आज भी सासों कि महक और लुक से हो जाते है turn on.

हम एसे क्यूँ हो जाते है कि जो हमें सुनता हैं !
हम उसपे अपना सब कुछ हार देते है !

बार बार हर बार हम यही वाली भूल क्यूँ कर देते है !
हम क्यूँ खोज में रहते है कि हमें कोई प्यार करे !

जब कि हम बहुत बार बहुत बहुत बार ये महसूस कर चुके है कि हमें सिर्फ़ हम ही पूरा कर सकते है !!

और हम क्यूँ अपने अंदर के सारे जज़्बात किसी के सामने रख देते है !
अपने घाव किसी और से क्यूँ मरहम करवाना चाहते है !

क्यूँ सुन ना चाहते है leave your self I will take care .
जब हमें पता होता है हम से ज़्यादा हमारी care कोई नही कर सकता !

क्यूँ अटक जाते है जब कोई कहता है "Give it all to me and don't say a word now "

क्यूँ लगता है ये सच है

हम इतने क्यूँ भुखे है प्यार के की कोई हाथ थामने कि बात करे तो हम रो देते है

Riddhi Gupta

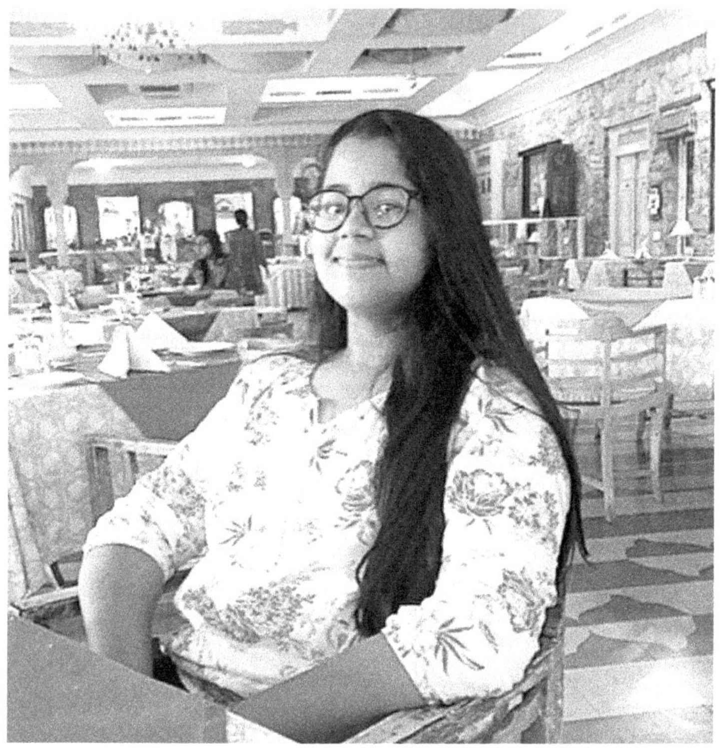

Riddhi is a Delhi based poet who is currently a student. She is utterly enthusiastic as well as zealous about writing poems and considers writing as a medium to express her thoughts and emotions. She is immensely fond of writing poems on nature. Along with that she is also passionate about clicking pictures that depict the beauty of our environment!
INSTAGRAM:- Thestargazingsouls

India Bharat

Resembling god's canvas
Where he's painted his greatest creation,
A country with such diverse cultures and languages,
It's an enigma of castes and religions.

निडर होकर लड़े थे सब,
जब बात आयी स्वतंत्रता के संग्राम की,
यहाँ कृष्ण की महिमा है, गीता की गरिमा है,
गाथाएँ यहाँ हर मनुष्य के कल्याण की।

In this sacred land of Ramayan and Mahabharat,
The greatest leaders and scientists took birth,
Even the soil here is so pure and divine,
It is indeed a paradise on Earth.

हिमालय से सुसज्जित मस्तिष्क है जिसका,
पावन गंगा जिसका अभिमान है,
भक्ति की अविरल धारा है जन-जन में प्रवाहित,
यह भूमि है जननी हमारी, हम इसकी संतान है।

To the world it might be just a country, developing and small,
But to me it's my world, my duty, my India, standing high and tall,
I am ready to sacrifice my life for this country any day,
Wishing this sacred country, A HAPPY INDEPENDENCE DAY!

Depression

Depression makes you lose faith in hope,
It makes you feel empty inside,
It deceives your mind and blurs it out,
Even though you had plenty of reasons to live, they all step aside.

The reality of depression isn't what many are aware of,
It's not just sitting in the corner and weeping all day,
Rather it's when someone is broken apart on the inside,
Yet they don't divulge their desolations, and smile anyway.

They feel they have no one to share their despairs with,
The thought of facing such struggles alone is indeed suffocating,
Their wails and yelps are left unheard,
Their breaths pounding, hearts trembling.

It forsakes our ability of realising the repercussions of our actions,
And even suicidal thoughts cross our minds,
But what about your parents who raised you?
Your self destruction might never let them smile.

What you all need to realise is that YOU ARE NOT ALONE!
Pour your heart out, we are there for you day and night,
Pursue your passion, happiness isn't so tough to obtain,
The dark clouds of gloom will surely fade out,
Bringing in the cheerful daylight.

So cherish every moment of life,
And let nothing destroy your inner charm,
Share your emotions even when you feel the slightest of discomfort,

You are your greatest treasure,
There is no place for self harm!

Depression is what abducted the lives of many,
We can't let it win anymore!
Share your sufferings with those whom you trust,
Just STAY BOLD and BELIEVE IN YOURSELVES to your very core!

Vedika Shukla

Vedika is an aspiring poet who is currently a student. She loves to express herself and connect with others through her writing. She also has a keen interest in photography and especially loves clicking pictures of the sky!

INSTAGRAM:- thestargazingsouls

Peace

Sitting on the ledge of the window,
I watch the rain drops pattering down,
As the smell of my chamomile tea soothes me down,
I let myself be consumed by the darkness surrounding me,
And in that moment I find myself at peace.

The World Within Me

And suddenly I zone out,
In the middle of the day whilst being surrounded by a hundred people,
I find myself in an all new world,
I can't really describe what I'm seeing,
It's like I'm in a world that's even beyond the unknown.

But the more I look around,
A sense of familiarity washes over me,
And I realize I'm nowhere else but in the magical world that's within me,
And I'm left utterly spellbound!

Pankaj Grover

Pankaj Grover is a good writer from Gidderbaha, Punjab. He is positive, kind, helpful, friendly person. He started writing in the Month of November,2018. He loves to write shayari and poem which topics family, love, friend, nature & many more.

INSTAGRAM:- heart_broken211199

बे-वफ़ा कहना सही नहीं होगा मेरे यार
क्या पता उसकी भी कोई मज़बूरी हो
प्यार तो वो भी बहुत करती थी मैं जानता हूं
शायद बीच राह में साथ छोड़ना उसके लिए जरूरी हो ।।

दिल की बातों को आज बोल दो
लगे जुबान पर ताले को आज खोल दो
कह दो की आपको भी मुझसे प्यार है
जिसका करना आपको आज इज़हार है ।।

दिखाकर पहले बढ़े बढ़े सपने
फिर ख़ुद ही तोड़ देते है
होते है आशिक़ कुछ ऐसे भी
जो बीच राह में ही छोड़ देते है ।।

हाल-ए-दिल

आंखों में छुपा रखा है जो प्यार
साफ साफ दिख रहा है मेरे यार
दिल अपने में दी जगह मगर
लफ़्ज़ों में ना कर सके हो ब्यान
चाहते हो बहुत मगर बता नहीं पाते हो
ये इश्क़ कमबख्त बढ़ा जानलेवा है साहब
इस से कभी दिल नहीं भर पाते हो
ये आंखों की नमी
बता देती है दिल की कमी
ना जाने कब होगा इश्क़ मेरा मुकमल
शायद बन ही जाए रुमाल मलमल
जिससे चेहरे पर होगा नूर
उसमें होगा बहुत सारा गरूर
जिसका होगा दिल साफ
वही थामेगा आपका हाथ ।।

Kirti Goel

Kirti Goel is a 15 years old ambitious girl. She is a class 9th student and She is from Ambala Cantt, Haryana. She is a passionate Poet who believes that words can make up the feelings!! She is the co-author of 20+anthologies out of which 15 has been published. She is the compiler of 5 books and is working on her solo book as well . She is also been regarded as the National Record Holder . Her pen name is Kalamqueen. And her evergreen lines from her quotes are...

"रिश्ते उम्मीद और जिंद पर टिकाए जाते है जनाब ,
खून का रिश्ता तो बस एक बहाना है"!

INSTAGRAM:- Kirtigoel24

Be The One Who Is Loved By Everyone

Let's change the phase of life,
Move ahead and start your drive!
Don't see what's happening beside,
Run and run but don't get behind!!

Let's get a start in this game of life,
Pick up all the adventures but don't stop your drive,
Make everyone extraordinary smile,
But don't forget to plan your time!!

Come on! let's find the key of lock,
Do work hard and open the mystery box!
Without any delay do Knock-knock.
Grab happiness from the open box.

Make your smile a great priority.
Because the happiness of your life depends upon your purity.
Be the one who is loved by everyone,
Because this precious life we get only once!!

So let's remove all the darkness and make this world a "Galaxy Of Goodness"

Anshuk Dwivedi'ranghin'

अठ्ठावीस वर्षीय अंशुक द्विवेदी'रंगहीन' श्रीमती उषा-डॉ. रमेश द्विवेदी की पुत्री है।मूलतः ग्राम धतुरिया,क्षिप्रा तट इंदौर(म.प्र.) भारत से है।वर्तमान में कनाड़िया,इंदौर में निवास करती है।हिंदी संस्कृत साहित्य से एम.ए. द्वयं करने के पश्चात बी.एड कर अध्यापन कार्य में प्रवत्त हैं।परम्परागत पारिवारिक ज्योतिषीय कार्य में संलग्न रहकर ज्योतिष कार्यालय संचालित करती हैं।इनके पोएटार्डस का संकलन "ज़ियारत" भी writersgramm appपर उपलब्ध है।छ अन्य सांझा काव्य संकलन"love without the knot, Treasure of love,SHE,A men's hidden emotions,प्रस्तावनाUnchained thoughts,The Wrinkle in time प्रकाशित हो चुके हैं।अन्य SHE The Mahakali,अहसास तेरे मेरे,last message,The tears we remember,वंदेमातरम,Aasma,Thrones and Roses,My love is gone,Roses and Souls,Rashmi,Hum Hindustani,Fog of Heart,Neacked Flower,The Versatile World,Euphoric World,long road to go,Tales of heart,EffectofEternity,SecretAdmirers, Nice&Spice,The Marked paper,The Gun in dusk,Battle of emotion,महा शिवाय में सह लेखिका के रूप में कार्य कर रही है।वर्ष २००४ से काव्य साधना में रुचि रखती है।इनकी कविताओं से जुड़ने के लिए इनके यूट्यूब चैनल#Anshukranghin से जुड़ा जा सकता है।

INSTAGRAM:- anshuk_ranghin

उसकी ख़ामोशी ने मेरा क़त्ल बड़ी ख़ामोशी से किया।
मेरे अश्क़ों ने शोर मचाया भी बहुत।
उसे हक़ था मेरा क़त्ल करने का,
उसने ये हक़ जताया भी बहुत।

मेरी ख़ामोश निगाहें उसके लरज़ते लब
ख़ुदा और क़यामत होगी कब।
जो बोल पड़े तो रुसवाई तू ही शोर की वज़ह
तू ही ख़ामोशी का सबब।

इतने ख़ामोश क्यूँ हो बता सकते हो,
कितने ऐब है मुझमें गिना सकते हो।
जाने दो परचम ए इश्क़ तले यूँ
ऐब ओ हुनर की जंग अच्छी नहीं होती।

ख़ामोशी रब की हो या लब की,
अश्क़ मज़हर होते हैं।
जिनके हिस्से में बोलती निगाहें हो,
हाँ वो ही अहलेज़र होते है।

Nilanjana Sarkar

Author Nilanjana Sarkar hails from West Bengal, Alipurduar and currently she's studying in class 12 and worked as an head of the Publication in WYIMUN on based on the three committee WHO, UNHRC and UNDP. She has also worked as an Entrepreneur with team Elite which deals with E-commerce, direct selling and social media platforms, she has already completed her internship in marketing by UNLEASH YOUR PASSION, she has been awarded as Extraordinary talent award on 2020 by Star and Genius book of record,her article had also get published and features over Indiatalks.org and yourstartups.in as a celebrity Author, she's is very hardworking and passionate girl and loves to do creativity through her writing, she mostly writes on erotics stuffs as well as on many topics which helps her to explore her more and more. She is a public speaker as well as a motivational speaker. She is an impulsive writer who oozes out her emotions and feelings and thoughts via writing.

INSTAGRAM:- _nilanjanaaa

Dear Love

To the sweetest person I know,
To the one with gleaming eyes and dazzling looks,
With a serene smile,
Which makes my day.
To the person with a golden heart
and burning passion for life.

Your love is the only thing I need,
And your smile is the medicine
for my illness.
I dream of none,
Except you.
Please stay besides me,
For all the good and bad times
We will tackle together,
I would love to hold you hand,
Forever, till my last breath.

I know,
I'm not the person you wished of,
And dreamt for.
I may not be your perfect partner in all ways.
But,
I'll always try my best,
To keep you happy and
see your cute innocent smile,
See you happy all the time,
Give all the hugs and cuddles you want,
Shower truck loads of love and affection.
And I promise,
That there will be not even a single day,
Of seeing tears in your eyes.
Last but not the least,
This is a promise,
For a lifetime.......

Arun Pratap Singh

This is Arun Pratap from Agra, and currently he is studying in third year bcom, he loves to write express his thoughts and emotions. He is very hardworking and loves to to express himself more and more through writings.

INSTAGRAM:- arun_pratap11

The Prison Of Love

My mind is blowing with pattern of scenarios,
scenarios that have put you to such trial.
Do you remember how i pleaded you as beggar,
our face punched with smiles as we ate the hamburger.

You fed me with care,
are breed so rare.
You re-energised my platelet's,
i can't forget your devotions,

You became the tower of my emotions.
And now your true love I can fess up.
My wish was only to see your face,
and look the judge got you to a new phase.

A phase of life imprisonment.
What do you think about such judgement?
Your life imprisoned to mine.
I know that was your most awaited chime.

And let me drive to you my wish,
In your life imprisonment your love to me always unleash.
Daily let's make scenarios till the end,
may the end be a new beginning.

May your trust stream always flow.
In my heart prison glow.
Before you get to these life imprisonment those were only my words
Remember you are my only world.

Meetu Chopra

मीतू चोपड़ा एक 25 वर्ष के युवती है, जो की जबलपुर, मध्य प्रदेश से सम्बन्ध रखती है |इनको कुछ नया लिखने का शौक हैं |ये अपनी कविताओं की वजह से कई प्रतियोगिता जीत भी चुकी हैं, इनको अभी '
आउटस्टैंडिंग कंट्रीब्यूशन इन एंथोलॉजी' से सम्मानित किया गया हैं, इनकी एक कविता तारे ज़मीन की मैगज़ीन में भी छाप चुकी हैं, ये भविष्य में बहुत से किताबें अपने नाम से छपवाने की इच्छुक हैं |
INSTAGRAM:- shayri_lover16

प्यार

प्यार वो नहीं,
जिसमें हर बार ई लव यू की जरुरत पड़े,
प्यार वो हैँ,
जिसमें बिना कहे ही सब समझ आये ...

प्यार वो नहीं,
जिसमें कोई जाति का शोर गूँजे,
प्यार वो हैँ,
जिसमें प्यार का खजाना लूटे...

प्यार वो नहीं,
जिसमें भेद रहे मया का,
प्यार वो हैँ,
जिसमें हर तरफ शोर हों भावनाओं का...

प्यार वो नहीं,
जिसमें तू या मैं का केद हों,
प्यार वो हैँ,
जिसमें सब हमारा हों...

प्यार वो नहीं,
जिसमें नज़र से घायल हों दो पल को,
प्यार वो हैँ,
जिसमें इंसान भूल जाये खुद को....

प्यार वो नहीं,
जिसमें रेस्टुरेंट में ही प्यार का रस नज़र आये,
प्यार वो हैँ,
जिसमें घर की दाल -रोटी में भी स्वाद आये.

प्यार वो नहीं,
जिसमें हम कागज़ की टुकड़ो पर हार जाये,
प्यार वो हैँ,
जिसमें हम मरने भी तेरी भहों में चाहें.

प्यार वो नहीं,
जिसमें गलतफमी का आसमान रिश्ते को तबहा कर जाये,
प्यार वो हैँ,
जिसमें खुशियाँ आसमान को छू जाये.

प्यार वो नहीं,
जिसमें नादानी का आइना उड़े हम निकल जाये,
प्यार वो हैँ,
जिसमें हम एक दूजे की कमजोरिओं का आदर कर पाये.

प्यार वो नहीं,
जिसमें रिश्ते बस दो लोगों तक हों,
प्यार वो हैँ,
जिसमें निभाना पूरे परिवार को हों...

प्यार वो नहीं,
जिसमें मीठे- मीठे प्रलोभन हों,
प्यार वो हैँ,
जिसमें हमदर्द हम हों....

प्यार वो नहीं,
जिसमें गुणों का स्वर सुनाई दे,
प्यार वो हैँ,
जिसमें हम प्रीत दिखाई दे.....

प्यार वो नहीं,
जिसमें शरीर का कोई काम हों,
प्यार वो हैं,
जिसमें एक दूजे को समझने की क्षमता हों....

प्यार वो नहीं,
जिसमें हम चॉक्लेट,केक से खुश हों,
प्यार वो हैं,
जिसमें हम तेरी मुस्कान के आगे कुर्बान हों....

प्यार वो नहीं,
जिसमें हम चोकीदार बने,
प्यार वो हैं,
जिसमें हम वफादार बने....

प्यार वो नहीं,
जिसमें हर समय मीठे बोली सुनाई जाये,
प्यार वो हैं,
जिसमें हर समय तकलीफ को अपनाया जाये...

प्यार वो नहीं,
जिसमें धन्यवाद का सुर काम भेजने लगे,
प्यार वो हैं,
जिसमें मित्रता की भावना का आनंद मिले...

प्यार वो नहीं,
जिसमें आँखों के काजल की प्यास हों,
प्यार वो हैं,
जिसमें हम तुम्हारे हवाले गिरफ्तार हों...

प्यार वो नहीं,

जिसमें ईर्ष्या का द्वार हों,
प्यार वो हैँ,
जिसमें खुशियों का साम्राज्य हों...

प्यार वो नहीं,
जिसमें तूँ मैं का जोश हो,
प्यार वो हैँ,
जिसमें सम्मान का उठता सैलाब हो.

प्यार वो नहीं,
जिसमें गुलाबों की पंखुड़ियां का मिलाप हो,
प्यार तो वो हैँ,
जिसमें काँटों से भरा बगीचा हो.

प्यार वो नहीं,
जिसमें हम शतरंज का खेल दिखाए,
प्यार वो है,
जिसमें दो आत्माओं का मिलाप हम गाये.

प्यार वो नहीं,
जिसमें हम वैलेंटाइन का प्रलोभन सुनाये,
प्यार वो हैँ,
जिसमें हम हर जन्म तुझे ही पाये.

प्यार वो नहीं,
जिसमें दूजे की पीड़ा भी अनसुनी हो जाये,
प्यार वो हैँ,
जिसमें हर मुश्किल में हम साथ निभाए.

Sonali Meher

Hey readers....!! She is Sonali Meher. From - Nuapada, Odisha, India. Currently pursuing for the degree of BAMS at Sri Sri nursingnath ayurveda medical College and RI. She is a Doctor by profession and writer by passion. She started writing when a very special moments come in her life and now for her writing is hobby. The writing is the 3rd person in that way of expressing their feelings, emotions and love. Now get a platform to exploring her writing. Hope ! You guys like it.

INSTAGRAM:- Sonalimeher124

तेरी बो मुस्कान
कितनी को मार डालती हैं ।।
तेरी बो नखरे
कितने को घायल करती हैं ।।
तेरी बो मासूम सी चेहरा
मुझे तेरे सामने झुक देती हैं ।।

हर दिल चाहता है
कोई एक ऐसा हो
जो आपके बिन कहे सारी बात को समझे ।।
आपके सूख दुःख हमेशा आपके साथ रहे ।।
कभी भी आपको बो अकेला
महसूस ना होने दें ।।

Dikshita Singh

Myself Dikshita Singh, i am from Uttar Pradesh and I believe in my own decisions and also I respect my love ones people but..I start writing because there is lots of things in my heart which is hidden behind lots of pressure...and now I want to express all the feelings in front of you peoples.

INSTAGRAM:- dik_shi_tasingh

मेरा सपना हो तुम

सनी अंखों का सपना हो तुम..
मेरे अबतक कि खुशियों का हिस्सा हो तुम...
मेरे जज़्बातों का अहसास हो तुम...
जिसकी बातों को सुनकर शर्म से मेरी आंखें झुक जाती है...
वो इकलौते इंसान हो तुम...
जिससे इतने कम वक्त में इतनी मोहब्बत हो गई मुझे
वो खुशकिस्मत इंसान हो तुम...
खुशकिस्मत इसलिए हो तुम क्यूंकि तुम्हे मै मिली एक
सच्ची मोहब्बत मिली...
मुझे तुम्हारे जैसा एक सच्चा इंसान मिला...
और इसलिए मेरे दिल का सबसे ख़ास हिस्सा हो तुम...
मेरी सच्ची मोहब्बत हो तुम...
मेरे ख्वाबों मै आकर युं सताया ना करो
मुझे हर छोटी बात पे डराया ना करो
माना मज़ाक मे बोलते हो कि चला जाऊ क्या
पर मै डर जाती हूं.. तुम्हे खोन से डरती हु
तुम्हारे होने से खुश रहती हूं...
ऐसे ही मुझपे प्यार लुटाया करो क्यूंकि
मेरा इकलौता सहारा हो तुम ।।

एक ख़्वाब

एक ख्वाब है मेरा की मेरी दिल की इकलौती धड़कन बानो तुम
मेरी लिखीं हर शब्दों का अहसास बनो तुम...
माना मेरा तुम्हे अपना सबकुछ मानना लाज़मी ना लगे तुम्हे
पर क्या करू इतना खूबसूरत अहसास जो देते हो..
मुझसे दूर रहकर भी मेरे पास रहना का अहसास जो देते हो..
पहले परेशान करके फिर इतने प्यार से जो मनाते हो..
मेरी हर छोटी बात ऐसे समझ जाते हो जैसे मेरे मन मे बसे हो...
हम मिले तो नहीं पर कई बार मिलने जैसा अहसास तुम हर रोज़ कराते हो...
इतनी जल्दी कौन इतने करीब आ जाता है यार जिससे एक पल दुर होने का मन नहीं करता...
इतने बिसी हो के भी वक्त मिलते हि तुरंत मुझे याद करते हो...
जानते हो कि तुम्हारी हर बात से शर्मा जाती हु...
फिर भी मेरा शर्माता चहरा देखने के लिए तुम बार बार वही बाते करते हो वही हरकते करते हो...
सुनो जब तुम यूं फोन पे से ही पास बुलाते हो.. जानते हो कि मेरी दिल की धड़कनें बढ़ जाती है पर उन्हे महसूस करने के लिए तुम बार बार अपनी खूबसूरत आवाज़ मे मुझे बुलाते हो..इतना सब करते हो ..अब तुम्हीं बताओ तुम्हे अपना सब कुछ न मानना
अपनी ज़िन्दगी ना बनाना ये मुझे लाज़मी नहीं लग रहा.. इसलिए मान लिया तुम्हे अपना सबकुछ...तो कभी जाना नहीं यूं मुंह मोड़ के मुझे सताना नहीं ।।

V.Dhanashree

Hello reader, she is V.Dhanashree from India living in the state called Tamilnadu in Chennai city. She is pursuing my undergraduate degree in History in Women's Christian College, Chennai, Tamilnadu. She is a simple and passionate writer who loves to write essays, poems and quotes in an easy and understandable manner so that it directly reaches the hearts of every reader. Her goal is to create a dignified society that spreads peace and kindness by eradicating poverty and illiteracy everywhere around the world. She strongly believes that writing is an extraordinary weapon to change the world to a better place to live in for all lives without any variations and discriminations.

The Incomparable Love

Before your birth, she carried you in her womb. After your birth, she carried you in her heart. She shows immense love towards you with all her care. She feeds you with joy and affection. She teaches you the goodness and strength of life with confidence. She makes you walk forward and she follows you behind. She is the guiding light and best care taker of your life. She is none other than a mother always. No love can be replaced to a mother's love in this world. We may go to different places and visit different people and relate with them. Many people will come and go in our life but they are not permanent. But none of them can selflessly love you till the end except your marvellous mother. She sacrifices her entire lifetime for her child's happiness and excellence. She is your strongest shield protecting you from all evils and dangers. She never takes care of herself but works tirelessly for the welfare of of her family. But have we ever paid back something to our indispensable mother? If not, then this is the right time to begin. Every mother wishes that her children must work hard to achieve their dreams. Your passion is always your mother's passion. So everyone who are reading this kindly start working on your dreams. Above all, as a son/daughter, it is your first and utmost duty to take care of your parents during their old age.

"Who can be a true love to you than a mother?"

Rushmi Raj.Amarthaluri

MS.Rushmi raj is a author and the poet.She is a student of B.pharm 3rd yr from guntur dist.An observational writer to write her creative thought's on paper and share them with as many people as she can. Hobbies like njoy the music, watching horror film's a lot, travelling & photography. Finally wants to be a grateful daughter to my lovely parent's..
INSTAGRAM:- Alone_gal_22

Journey of Love

Everyday that passes
I feel that, I love you more
I feel thankful for the times we spend together
I know and feel that you are my perfect companion & friend
And i would choose you again...
and again... & again...!
Naturally we have difficult moment's
But i would not give up even these
Because it's a part of the journey of love
That we've been on
I want to travel by your side...forever
Because,I love you...

Babee Boo

I still remember the feeling i felt when i first started talking to you my prince..
You have touched the deepest chords of my heart & soul with your pure and pristine love. I want to love you back in a million ways with all i have. I want to be my entire world & I want my to revolve around you. You are the only one who deserves to stay in my heart till eternity. I will always treasure you like my most precious treasure and I'll never let you go. Since the day I've met you, I've been living in a magical trance and every single moment i have spent with you is mesmerizing and magical. Every moment that we spent together is a treasure of my heart and soul. You have filled my life with immense love that my heart and soul brimming with love for you. I want to spend the rest of my life in your arms... I want to sleep by hugging you and wake up in your arms and stay by your side till my last breath. My soul will stay entwined with your soul forever..

Sabene Rizvi

Sabene Rizvi was born in New York, USA. Her writing career started when she was eight years old and wrote her first story called The Picnic. She then went on to publish 35 short story books online on https://www.storyjumper.com and 42 stories in Young Nation, a weekly magazine of Daily Nation. She discovered her love for poetry during the Covid-19 pandemic lockdown. She joined literary communities online and made friends with emerging intellectuals. She also published seven chapters of her first novel on https://www.wattpad.com and is currently completing it. She lives with her loving mom, cat and dog.

INSTAGRAM:- poetrybysabene_

One last letter

Hi,
It's me again. The annoying one. I have one last letter for you. Let's begin shall we?

Words cannot describe the pain you have caused me. From abusive situations to bullying, you never cared. Did you? Crushing my hopes and dreams. Giving me trust issues, anxiety, depression. You did all of it. Broken bones healed with time but what about what was broken on the inside. You broke it further. Nay, you broke it first. Trauma. Hurt. Pain. Anxious sleepless nights. Nail biting. Fear of letting others down. Losing hope. You caused all of it but I thank you. Thank you for showing me what the world truly was at such a young age. Your people say I'm really mature for my age. Thank you for putting me through that pain because it was through that pain that I found myself. Found myself in the darkest corner, crippled on the floor. Pulled myself out of it, out of my mind. For nothing ruins iron more than it's own rust. Thank you for making me a warrior. A warrior who made herself a weapon.
Goodbye,
May we never meet again.

Somya Tyagi

Somya Tyagi is a 20 yrs old ambitious girl. She is a medical student and she is from sambhal up.
She loves writing as writing is her passion.
She is the co-author of 50+ anthologies.
She is the compiler of the 16 books.
She is the HR MANAGER and PROJECT HEAD in The Opus Coliseum publication.
She is the Magazine Head of TRIDESTA MAGAZINE.
She is the NATIONAL AND WORLD RECORD HOLDER.
And her evergreen lines from her quotes are...
"Kuch baten jo juba na kh pay,
Bs alfaz milkr shayri m utar jay.
INSTAGRAM:- dil_ki_bateen

मैं सोना तो चाहती हूं अपने अधूरे
सपनो को पूरा देखने के लिए।।
पर उनको हकीकत बनाने का
जुनून मुझे इतनी जल्दी सोने नही देता।।

हाल अब इस दिल का कैसे बताए,
जूबा तो है पर लफ्ज़ ना मिल पाए।
की कुछ इस तरह खाली सा हो गया है दिल,
की अब मरना भी चाहे तो मौत ना आए।

Mani Prasad Kar

Mani Prasad Kar lives in Jajpur. He is a person who loves to live his dreams . He is an emerging writer, a poet, a memer , and a free living guy . In his writings one can feel his emotions and visualize the words. He wishes to publish his own novel some day. He wants people to sense the aura of humanity and love through his writings. He looks forward for love from his readers .
INSTAGRAM:- Zephyr_of_woe

A Cup Of Coffee

"Waiter! A Cup of coffee please" a voice called for,
There was he, sitting looking at the setting sun and the sea roar.
A cool Zephyr entangling a balmy music brushed by his face,
His eyes looking up at the evening birds pace.
A tear drop fell adoring his eyes,
All those promises she had made were just lies.
A memory enfolded him to the time they were together,
He was sitting on the same table with her.
Romantic chords were buzzing,
It was an evening akin.
It was there day of love,
"Sir! your coffee " a voice pulled him back to senses with a shove.
He imbibed a little of it.
The coffee still tastes the same he smiled in wit.
The smoke from the coffee tugged him again to his memories,
He was lost in her eyes as if they were telling beautiful stories.
He still remember the coffee making her a cute moustache print.
And how they laughed when he gave her this hint.
He could reminisce him kneeling down on the beach sand,
Proposing her with a ring in his hand.
"Will you marry me !" he said
He could recite how her eyes gleamed with tears of love and how she blushed to red.
He still remember her warm tight hug,
The moment was cute as a bug.
She held his hand softly,
And said we will always be together with a smile comely.
She said "Happy Anniversary dear!"
what a humor! The girl who promised to walk hand in hand is not near.
He is still at this place today,
Even after years celebrating her long forgotten special day.
He smiled to his thoughts of irony
And he called the waiter to cut the bill in the name of "Mani".

Pratham Mittal

He is very Positive, kind, helpful, friendly and happy soul. His passion is painting and writing. He has won many competitions, He has Been Co-Authored of 75+ Anthology and He has Been Compiler of 15+ Anthologies, and in the Process for more. He is an OMG Books Of Record Holder + Bravo International Book of World Record Holder for his Anthology Speaking My Truth. Participated in International Writing Competitions and Featured in Many Magazines & Newspaper also.

A Child

A child is born in pink
A bundle of white fur deep in wink
Plays with all the greens in park
Which always brings them many spark.
When a toddler sees something Red
Don’t know why he feels so glad?
Blue is in fashion
Everybody's passion
Summer sets in Yellow
Making all eyes follow
Violet comes with a twinkle
Oh Clouds! let the raindrops sprinkle
White is so pure n calm
Feels so good on my open palm.
Colours of Life brings memories to all or any
Let us cherish them n make them tall.

Chirag L Sagar

Chirag L Sagar is a 1st year MBBS student studying at Srinivas Institute of Medical Sciences and Research Centre,Mangalore. His hobbies are poetry, reading - books,novels, autobiographies,philately, listening to songs,sports like cricket and badminton,cooking. He is a medico by profession and a writer by passion. His dream is to become an Oncologist and a successful writer.

INSTAGRAM:- chirag_cls18

A Conspiracy of Life

Life had conspired,
It helped me fulfil my unheard dreams.
My prayers had a broken base,
I'm clueless how it reached out to you.
How did you even apprehend my silence ?
My obsession has brought me close to you.
Is it your mercy ?
My obsession changed my destiny.
Your love is my obsession,
Oh, my lord !
My desires were ignited slowly,
Wishes buried deep in my heart were stifling.
Carried through to you in a smolder,
I have scratched the threshold of madness,
Oh my lord !
This obsession of mine,
Is your benevolence.
This delusion of mine,
Is my love towards you !
Some desires burnt slowly.
Displayed the pain, deep within my heart,
I was agonizing in the cafe of my memories,
Oh, my lord !
My dreams have set me free,
My destiny changed due to your love

Flairs and Glairs, a platform by a student for the students. We are esteemed youth struggling to carve out our path for our future and we follow a basic mindset Since everyone is not born with all-round skills. Joining hands with people who are born to execute it with perfection is the best way to evolve. Self-Evolution is the need of the hour but, evolving as a community is what we strive for. The initiative as kickstarted by, Founder- Mr. Shubham Shah with the motive to utilize the skillset and talent of writing has now a team of 10+ people who are actively participating into newer forms of learning and discovering talents among youngsters. We Provide platform and services like Publishing opportunities, Open mics, Workshops, Hands-on training. Operating with Brand Name of Flairs and Glairs (Publication House), we offer the chance of elevating a passionate writer to an esteemed author With Brand name Teekhe Zasbaaat. We bring to you an opportunity to get accustomed with the Public Speaking and Presenting of Thoughts along with regular challenges to brush up your inking spirit. The newest initiative to extend our services we introduced in a new writing Platform- The Glittering Fables and Ink Over Tears.

We Choose to Fly Like A Falcon than to be

a Leg Pulling Crab.

www.ingramcontent.com/pod-product-compliance
Ingram Content Group UK Ltd.
Pitfield, Milton Keynes, MK11 3LW, UK
UKHW022003190726
13853UKWH00004B/1715